Devils in the Dark

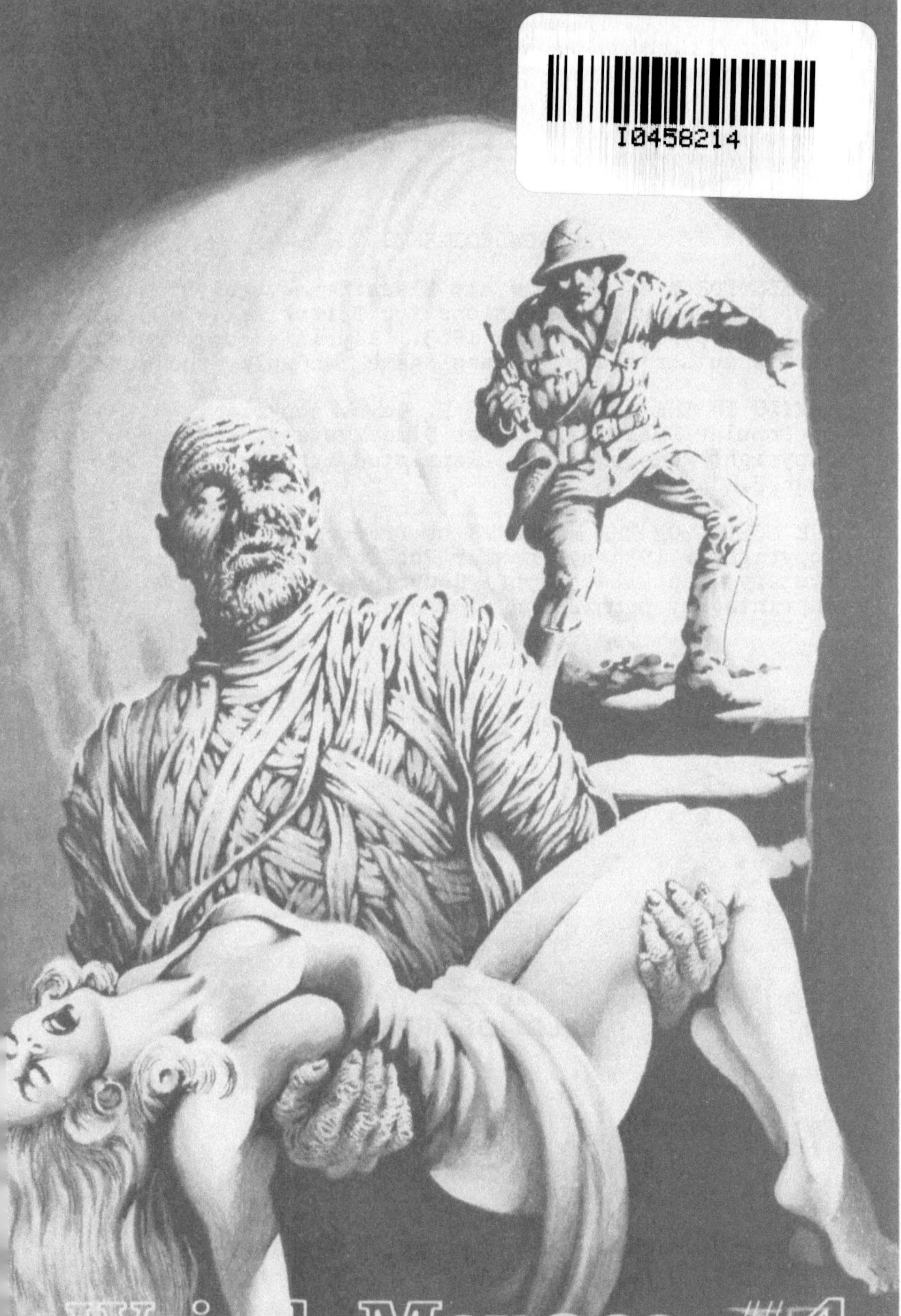

Weird Menace #4

DEVILS IN THE DARK - WEIRD MENACE CLASSICS # 4
$5.50 per copy

Edited and published by Robert Weinberg, 10606 S. Central
Park, Chicago, Il. 60655

ACKNOWLEDGMENTS

MODELS FOR MADNESS by Wyatt Blassingame, copyright ©
1935 by Popular Publications for Terror Tales, December
1935. Copyright renewed 1963. Reprinted by permission
of the author's agen, Blassingame, McCauley and Wood.

DEVILS IN THE DARK by Hugh B. Cave, copyright © 1934
by Popular Publications for Dime Mystery, February 1934.
Copyright Renewed 1962. Reprinted by permission of
Hugh B. Cave.

THE COMING OF THE MAD ONES by Frederick C. Davis,
copyright © 1936 by Popular Publications for Dime
Mystery, September 1936. Copyright renewed 1964.
Reprinted by permission of Frederick C. Davis

FIRST EDITION

WILDSIDE PRESS

CONTENTS

This issue is dedicated to
Frederick C. Davis, whose
work will be remembered with
fondness by all pulp fans.

CHAMBER OF HORRORS

It is with great regret that we note that this issue
of WEIRD MENACE will be the last to feature a story
by Frederick C. Davis. Mr. Davis passed on late last
year and this was the last story whose rights we bought
from him. In many ways, we feel it is one of his best
and we only regret he is not alive to see its repub-
lication. Mr. Davis was always encouraging and com-
plimentary towards all of our efforts in the pulp
revival, and he will be missed.
By now, you will have noticed our change in cover for-
mat. While we liked reprinting old weird-menace pulp
covers, we were being told by dealers who handle our
reprints that the books looked too much the same. So,
we are pleased to report that Steve Fabian, probably
the premier black-and-white artist in the fantasy field
will be doing the covers for this series of Weird Menace
reprints. None of the covers will illustrated stories,
as was the case with many of the original pulps, but will
instead reflect the series title - Weird Menace! We
think this first cover to be a real gem and can't wait
to see what the future holds.
As is often the case, the real world has far outstripped
our stories with horror stories - from the mass murders
in Jonestown to the gruesome sex slaying in the Chicago
suburban area. For those who doubt the believability of
the stories we offer here, just look at the headlines.

This issue, for a change, we have reprinted three long
stories from the weird-menace pulps - three of the
very best in our opinion. The long novelet (or short
novel) gave the author of such work the room to develop
mood and complicate plot that no short story ever does.
Each of these stories features madness - soul seering
madness that seems to creep and crawl and slowly threaten
to engulf the characters. Time and space is needed to
create such a mood and we feel that the short novel is
the perfect length for the weird-menace story. Your
comments on this would be greatly appreciated.
Next issue is already completely laid out and we hope
to better our record of being nearly six months late
with this one by being close to on time with that.
Seheduled is some very fine work including an author
who has never before appeared in this reprint series.
We think it will be a winning number, especially with
another fine Fabian cover.
Now, lock the doors and turn on all the lights for these
are not stories to be read alone and in the dark....

                         Robert Weinberg
                         Editor & Publisher

MODELS for MADNESS

Jim Farlan, maker of waxen murder-figures, found his skilled hands mysteriously soaked with the blood of fiendishly murdered people, whose features he saw in those of his statues. . . . And he knew not how to avert still another eerie, gruesome slaying, when again there appeared in his handiwork the countenance of a living person—this time the face of Neta Phillips, the girl he loved . . . !

TIME passes very slowly in the narrow cell of the death house. There is no clock, no way to judge the creeping minutes except by the occasional meals which the guards bring, ⁚ ⁚ by the slow crawl of the sunlight through

6

By Wyatt Blassingame
(Author of "Monster from the Mists," etc.)

MURDER OF
CHATAHIELIAN
APRIL 5, 19

the barred windows and across the cement floor. During the long hours of the night I lie awake and hear time drag past with a cruel and terrific slowness. Four more days and four more nights I must stay here; then they will lead me down the short corridor that stretches into eternity.

The big, blank-faced chair, the electrodes on leg and head, the furious hum of the current and my body lunging against the straps that hold it. Another murderer gone. . . . I shall be glad, glad when those four days and nights are over. For even here, alone, barred off from the world, I am afraid.

I am not trying to beg for mercy. I don't want to live—now. This will not be read until after my death. It is partially

7

to help pass the time that I write, and also because I want those whom I leave behind to understand as much as is possible. God knows, I don't understand fully, but I do know that I didn't commit these murders wilfully, and that no matter what horrors I performed with my hands I never wanted to do them.

More than this no one will be able to understand. That's why I would not help the lawyer which the court forced me to have at my trial; that's why I pleaded guilty and refused to answer questions. I didn't want to kill those persons, and yet. . . . Now it is best that I walk down that short corridor into the small room with the large chair—and into eternity.

You will comprehend more fully if I start with the dream. It is a dream which has haunted me and torn at my nerves until I was half mad with terror, has held me trembling through long fear-whipped hours of darkness. It haunts me even now, in this cell where I can reach no one. My hands are big and strong enough to take a human throat and rip the windpipe from it, but they cannot shake these bars through which the sunlight streams in slanting, mote-filled beams. And I am glad. . . .

THE dream came to me the night before the first murder. It was too horribly real to be a dream and I sat up in bed suddenly, my body wet with perspiration. For a moment I couldn't breath because of the terror that cut into my chest like an icy wire. That couldn't have been a dream, I thought. It couldn't! It was like a picture flashed in the darkness. It was like. . . . And then, although I have never understood how, I knew what it was. I never meant to say the words, but I heard my own voice muttering them into the darkness.

It was as if the night had split for one moment letting me see into the future!

I can't explain that feeling. I have never put much faith in dreams, but in the first instant I *knew* I had looked into the Great Tomorrow. This was what added so much to the sickening terror of the dream itself. I can't explain *how* I knew it, but I want anybody who reads this to understand that I *did* know it. The truth simply was in my mind from the first, though for days I tried to tell myself that I was being absurd. But all the time I *knew.*

I can see the dream now as plainly as I did when I sat bolt upright in my bed, cold and shaking. I can see my own face, distorted almost into bestial savageness and with the eyes so squint as to be like those of an Oriental; I can see my big body hunched over Neta Phillips, her slender waist cradled in my left arm, her dark hair flowing loose. And I can see my right hand tearing her throat like a steel claw, ripping out the windpipe, see the wild spurt of the blood and the savage, scarlet rivulets flowing down toward her breasts.

In the second while the dream lasted I was aware also of a peculiar odor. Perhaps I use the wrong word when I say "odor," because it wasn't actually a smell; but it more nearly touched on that than any other sense. It was the sensation, the feeling that a person gets on entering a home in China where one family has lived for hundreds of years, where, within the very walls of the house, and in the air you breathe, you become aware of history, of the quiet ghosts of unforgotten ages. Somehow, in the first horrible moment of dreaming, I became aware of such an odor.

"It was just a dream," I told myself, and I lay back. But I couldn't sleep. It seemed absurd that I should be so afraid of a dream. I tried to laugh at the idea of

8

my charming Neta Phillips. I believed then that I was going to marry Neta; that there was nothing on God's earth that I wanted so much. Even now it shakes me to remember how I loved her. There were times while she stood spotlighted in front of the orchestra and sang, that I had to grip my table, to keep from getting up and catching her in my arms and shouting to the world that I loved her, loved her! So you can understand how absurd the idea of killing her would seem.

But I couldn't forget it. I kept lying there thinking about the dream, and about the way my eyes had looked. Not like my own at all, but slant and terrible as those of a Chinese demon. And I remembered the peculiar Oriental odor which had come with the dream, and I got to thinking about Tai Ming.

A YEAR before, at the university where I was doing some graduate art work on a scholarship—and Neta was finishing her senior year—we had known Tai. A quiet, studious young man with all the education the West could give him, and with the exquisite politeness of the Orient, he had amused Foster Duncan and me by the seriousness with which he worshipped his ancestors. Foster had suggested that I draw the caricatures of Tai and all his family. Neta had urged me not to, but I did anyway.

We were in Tai's apartment when I showed them to him. I shall never forget the change which came over his face. One moment it was bland, smiling, almost Occidental. The next it was contorted in savage and terrible fury and his eyes were those of a Chinese fiend. But the snarl had lasted only a moment. After that his face was quiet, and passive, and utterly without expression. His voice was as smooth as silk, and flat. He was coldly, silently furious at the humorous drawings of the members of his family.

"You have insulted a thing more precious than life, not only to me, but to my entire family; to those who have not yet been born and to those who have been dead for hundreds of years. It is an insult that we do not forget." And in that same flat, silky voice he went on to swear revenge in words that were beyond retracting.

I had tried to apologize then, seeing how seriously he took the joke. He had only bowed and held open his door. I remember that last glance of his room as I went out. It was the average room of an American college boy, strictly Occidental; and yet, in the very air which pervaded the place, there was something weird and Oriental and inescapable.

That was a few days before commencement, and I never saw him again. I hadn't thought of him for several months until the night of the dream. For a long while I lay there thinking of him and of Neta and of the way Foster Duncan had laughed at the joke. I tried to keep thinking of them so that I could shut the dream from my mind. But I couldn't.

Finally I got up and switched on the lights. "A deep drink of bourbon will put me to sleep," I thought. When I reached for the bottle I saw the faint blue lines on the back of my hand, blinked against the light and looked at them more closely. They were barely visible and tangled, almost like a Chinese letter. "Must have been sleeping, with my hand pushed against a wrinkle in the sheet," I thought. Then I took a stiff drink of the whiskey and forgot about it.

It was the next night at the club called Death's Roadhouse that the whole thing was recalled, horrible and unforgetable, to my mind.

My uncle, Wade Farlan, owns and operates the roadhouse. It hadn't been doing so well under the name of The Silver Moon when he bought it. He had changed the name to Death's Roadhouse, and filled the place with wax models of famous murders. I think the only reason he bought the place was to have a chance to out-do the Dead Rat Cabaret in Paris, a place which held a strange fascination for him. The idea had appealed to the tired and wealthy of the city. They flocked there nightly, partially for the weird atmosphere, partially to hear Neta Phillips sing. I had agreed to do the gruesome decorations and the models, and help him with the roadhouse, simply because my work as a sculptor hadn't proved as good as I thought it would—and I wasn't earning a living.

The lights in Death's Roadhouse are a dim and ghastly green that flickers constantly. The orchestra is hidden behind palms, and makes a specialty of weird, wailing music. Around the walls, scattered among the tables, even on the dance floor, are the wax statues; and I think I did a good job on them. For they were terrible enough by daylight, and in the dim, ever wavering illumination of the place they seemed to move, to be in the very act of murdering one another. A man splitting a woman's head with a hatchet; another ripping his wife's throat with a razor; a nude woman on her hands and knees, with a knife still seeming to quiver in her back. . . .

THE night after the dream I was sitting at a corner table with Neta when Foster Duncan dropped in and joined us. It was several minutes before Neta's specialty number was to begin—a wailing, gruesome song that packed the roadhouse nightly. I have always wondered how Neta could sing that number, it was so entirely different from her quiet, lovable nature. While we were waiting the conversation got around to college somehow, and Neta said, "I had a letter from Tai Ming today. He's gone back to China."

At first I didn't know why the mention of Tai's name should frighten me so. Then I remembered I had been thinking of him the night before; and the dream came back to me like thunder. I had to fight my nerves to steadiness before I asked, "What did he have to say?"

Neta looked at me curiously, her level, dark eyes opening wide. For a moment she glanced at Foster, then back to me. "What's the trouble with both of you? You look as if you had seen a ghost."

I turned to Foster, who is a lanky, rather gaunt man with a sense of humor that is liable to take a cruel turn. His mouth was twitching slightly, but as I looked at him he controlled it and began to laugh. "I've never quite got over the way he cursed us about those pictures you drew. He said he was going to have revenge, and he meant it."

Whenever Neta smiled there was a sudden light in her dark eyes. "You don't have to worry about that any more. That's why he wrote me. He said he was sorry about the rumpus he raised; that he should have known that neither of you meant any insult. It was a very polite, nice letter."

"That's bad," Foster said. "A Chinaman apologizes for stepping behind you just before he sticks a knife in your back." He tried to make his voice sound as if he were joking, but there was a nervous, jagged edge to it.

I opened my mouth to say that I had been thinking about Tai the night before, but stopped when I saw Roger Swanson coming between the tables and scattered statues. It was too dim in the place to distinguish his features, but I recognized him by the sleek cut of his clothes and the gliding way he moved.

He paused beside our table, scowling at me. In the glow from the green lamps, his blond hair took on a sickening color and his thin, rather handsome face seemed to twist with the wavering of other lights.

"You might get up and see if there is any work for you to do," he said. "And it's about time for Neta's number. The orchestra leader was asking for her." He wheeled and walked away from us, a slim, too-immaculate figure among the statues of death.

Foster turned his gaunt head and looked after him. "The collar ad doesn't seem to care for either of you," he remarked.

I said, "He's my cousin, but there's little love between us. He took law at school, though my Uncle Paul—the eccentric old millionaire who lives with one servant out on Woodley Road—knew he'd never be able to win a case, and took mercy on him, made him his secretary or something. It must be hell on Uncle Paul. He hates everybody, except maybe Neta; and he hates Roger worse than all the others put together. But blood's blood in my family, and so he gave Roger the job. And Uncle Wade lets him do some publicity work for the roadhouse."

"How is your Uncle Paul?" Foster asked. "I haven't heard you mention him in more than a year."

"I haven't been to see him in two or more. He lives shut up with his books and one servant. Roger is his only connection with the world, and I don't envy him that one. He doesn't want visitors."

"I knew an old duck like that once. He. . . ." But suddenly I did not hear Foster's voice; I did not hear the muted wailing of the orchestra or the dulled murmur of voices from other tables. I was conscious of no sound at all, of nothing except an odor that was more a *feeling* than an odor—the feeling of ancient, Chinese homes heavy with history and ancestry worship. . . .

IT WAS the smell I had sensed last night, just before I dreamed I had

murdered Neta. All at once that picture flashed horribly clear in my mind. I could see her black hair swaying about her face, see my big hand at her torn throat, almost feel the fingers wet with blood.

And in that same instant I saw it!

The statue was not twenty feet from us, close to the wall, and half hidden by banked palms. Somehow I hadn't noticed it before, but then, all at once, I was staring at it. Slowly my mouth began to open, muscle began to ache along my jaw and my eyes grew wide with terror.

I felt Neta's hands on my arm, shaking me, heard her voice thin and shrill. "Jim! What is it? What's wrong?" But I never looked at her. I couldn't take my eyes from the statue.

The shifting green lights flickered on it through the palms so that it seemed to quiver with heavy breathing. But it was not that which held me. It was the horror of the figures themselves.

It was the statue of a large, wide shouldered fellow holding a smaller man with his left arm, while with his right hand he ripped out the man's throat. And in the long, furious instant that I stared, I knew that the contorted face of the killer was my own face!

I didn't hear anything then, didn't feel anything except the cold terror starting deep in me and rising like a black flood. The wild, unexplainable sensation of looking into the future struck me, froze my veins into jagged icicles. I came half erect, gripping the table, shaking it. My eyes bulged, fixed on the face which was a horrible mask of my own face.

"It's only wax," I thought. "Someone is playing a joke on me. That's all. A. . . ." But then the dream was clear in my mind again: the picture of Neta held exactly as this man was held, her throat torn open as his was, and my own face, with the eyes of a Chinese demon, exactly the same.

11

My gaze shifted to the face of the victim. There was something familiar about that face, though it was twisted with unbearable agony—the mouth open so that I had the wild impression that it didn't scream, only because the sound had been torn from its throat a second before.

And then, at a table just to the left of the statue, I saw the man who was modeled as the victim!

He was in dinner clothes, seated opposite a pretty blonde girl who was leaning toward him, grasping his arm. But his eyes were on the statue, wide and terrified. He was unmoving as the wax images, and his face was ghastly under the lights.

I don't remember getting up from the table. From that time on the whole thing was like a black dream; I can never be sure how much of it I remember and how much a furious and terrified imagination has created since. I only know that I was going toward the wax models, my hands stretched out in front of me, thinking: "I'll touch them; I'll prove they are only wax, and then. . . ."

When the lights went out I don't know. I didn't hear any of the confusion, the wisecracks shouted into the dark, the women giggling hysterically. It seemed to me that I was gradually being absorbed by the darkness as I pushed my way through it. And I knew that I was swerving toward the table where the man in dinner clothes sat with the blonde. Something was pulling me toward him while I fought to keep away, to go toward the statues, instead. I struggled with every fading ounce of my strength, but somehow I swerved more and more toward the table.

Perhaps I screamed then; perhaps it was the man or the girl he was with who screamed. All I remember is the high and terrible cry jangling in the darkness. . . .

CHAPTER TWO

Hands of Blood

THE light seemed to have been around me a long time before I became aware of it. I was standing erect, doing something with my hands that I didn't understand, and there was a steady, liquid sound in my ears. Then, with a slow, sure rush, consciousness came back to me.

I was in the lavatory of the roadhouse, scrubbing my hands. A steady stream of water splashed into the marble washbowl and gurgled down the drain. It was in the water that I first saw the faint red coloring. And then I looked at my hands. . . .

For a long while I stood there staring at them. I didn't breath, because my lungs were cold and rock-hard against my ribs; my mouth was open, but I didn't make any sound. I could feel my eyes aching against their sockets, and in my mind was the picture of those statues, of the blood gushing from a torn throat, of myself swerving in the dark toward the table where the living image of one of those statues sat.

What happened after that I could not remember. But thick between my fingers was the dark smear of blood! And underneath the blood the blue lines that were like a Chinese letter showed plainly!

I must have stood there a full minute before I became aware of the chaos bursting in the dining room. Men were shouting, women screaming, tables crashing over. And then, suddenly, above it all, I heard the voice of my Uncle Wade sound like thunder. "Be calm! No one's going to leave here before the police come!"

Somehow I finished washing my hands, quickly and thoroughly—but the blue lines would not come off. Somehow I forced myself to go back into the dining room, where I didn't know what I would find. I tried to keep my mind blank, but pictures burst like shells in my brain so that I staggered as I walked. Why had that blood been on my hands? How did I get in the washroom? Why was the whole roadhouse in such a terrified uproar? I didn't want to guess at the answers, and yet I couldn't keep from it. What had happened in those seconds of blackness I didn't know.

The green, wavering lights were on when I slid past the palms into the dining room. In the nasty glow the wax statues seemed more alive than the human beings, but I was not interested in any statue but one. Between me and the place it stood, every person in the roadhouse had gathered in a circle. They were all looking at something on the floor, and none of them saw me.

Over the heads of the crowd I could see my Uncle Wade in the center, his mane of white hair pushed back from his forehead, his dark eyes burning. All the men in my family are large, but Uncle Wade is the biggest of the lot, and the hardest, despite his fifty years. He was bellowing orders to his men, and waiters were jumping toward exits. His voice rode high over the hysterical sobbing of the women. A man in front of me turned away quickly, his hand over his mouth, as though he were about to get sick. Beyond him, I could see the floor in the middle of the circle.

I didn't cry out because I couldn't. All the while I had known what would be there, though I had tried not to admit it even to myself. Now the sight struck me like a fist in my stomach, and I rocked backward, my mouth open as though there were not enough air in the room for me; and yet I could not breathe.

Flat on his back at my uncle's feet was the man toward whose table I had

swerved in the dark. The green light twitched across him, but he was still, horribly still except for the slow-widening blood under his face.

His whole throat was gone, as though the windpipe had been ripped out with a gigantic hand! The torn flesh hung in jagged ribbons, and the blood drooled from it in unceasing streams!

FOR what seemed ages I stood there, sick with a terror that was beyond comprehension. And starting deep inside me, rising into my brain with the slow, furious pressure of my blood, came the dream. I had seen a statue of this man and of me ripping out his throat. Now he was dead. *And I had dreamed of murdering Neta!*

Fear was a cold agony crushing my mind. Through it came the sound of muffled voices that I heard without understanding. Uncle Wade was bellowing, "Every one go back to their tables and wait for the police."

A woman was saying over and over, "Oh, God. It's real. He's really dead. He's really dead."

A man asked, "Who is he? I saw him sitting there, and then the lights went out and when they came on, he. . . ."

Another voice said, "It's John McDavid. He's the fellow who's been doing the stories the critics all rant about."

The deep voice of my uncle boomed, "Go to your tables!" The command crashed into my brain like a whip-lash and I turned, reeling, toward the corner where I had been sitting with Neta and Foster Duncan.

Persons were passing on all sides, but no one noticed when I stopped. I couldn't go any farther. Every muscle in my body shook with terror and wild impulses slashed counterwise through my brain. A long while I stood there, gaping at the spot where the statue had been.

"God!" I whispered. "Great. . . ." I couldn't say any more because there was no air in my lungs, and my ribs were crushing inward.

The statues, with my face and the face of John McDavid had vanished. In its place was one of the wax figures I had modeled.

I turned slowly, staring about the room. There was no doubt of it—this was the place. But the statue I had seen a short while ago was not there. I had the eerie feeling that it had never been there, except in my imagination. It had been no more real than the dream, a brief rent in the curtain of the future! And if one of them had come true, then the other. . . . Oh God! I put both hands over my eyes and stood there, swaying.

Something plucked at my arm and I turned to face Neta. "Jim, where have you been? What was wrong when—" She stopped, staring into my eyes.

Looking at her I felt terror like a living agony inside me. My gaze took in her full, soft mouth, the dark hair that framed her face, her slender, curving figure—and seeing her I saw the dream like a wall of flame and horror between us.

"Let's go to the table," I said huskily, and went toward it. I was unconscious of the room about me, of the noises, of everything except this horror which had taken place, and of the terrible picture which lived in my imagination: Neta, her throat torn as McDavid's had been, the dark blood streaming down onto her breasts.

Foster Duncan was not at the table.

Neta pulled her chair close to me, took my big hands in her small ones. "Now tell me," she whispered. "What happened to you? You're not hurt, not . . .?"

I looked at her, and felt love roll over me like a great wave. And there was courage in knowing I loved her so much. Surely I couldn't harm her. I tried to tell myself that the whole thing was crazy.

After the lights went out something or somebody had killed McDavid and struck me in passing, knocking me momentarily unconscious. At college I had played a whole quarter of a football game and never been able to remember it. That was what had happened tonight.

Then I thought of the statue. How in God's name could I explain it?

"Neta,"—the words hurt my throat when I spoke—"did you notice. . . ." I turned my eyes away from her, afraid for her to see the terror jerking in my face. "Did you notice that statue? Did you see anything . . .?"

Her hands tightened on mine, tried to pull me around—but I kept looking away from her. "Which one?" she asked. "I haven't noticed any new ones. Why?"

I swung to face her then, my jaw set hard. "There was one near the table where McDavid sat. Did you . . .?"

A new look came into her eyes now, a slow, growing shadow of wonder and doubt and fear. It was a long moment before she turned to glance at the statue I indicated. "It's been there all evening," she said. "What's wrong with it?"

I didn't answer her. I don't think my face had changed; for her words had frozen me, stopped the very beating of my heart until it hung cold as a stone inside me. No one had seen the statue, with my face and the face of the dead man—except he and I. Now he was dead with his throat ripped apart. *And there had been blood on my hands!*

"It was never there," I thought. "Never there except in my mind and his. We were seeing into the future, and the dream I had of Neta. . . ."

IT WAS several minutes later that Foster Duncan came back to the table. I don't remember anything he had to say, and the police investigation is a vague blur in my mind. What had happened in those moments of darkness? How had the blood got on my hands, and why had I slipped away to wash it off? The questions thundered over and over through my brain.

The police, I remember vaguely, went over the roadhouse from end to end. They reenacted the crime, keeping us in our former seats. But neither Foster Duncan nor Neta mentioned the fact that I had been out of my chair, going in the direction of McDavid, when the lights went out. No one else seemed to have noticed. So the police learned nothing, and at last they let us go home.

I didn't sleep that night. It seemed to me that if I shut my eyes, the dream would come crashing back into my mind —and I was afraid. I tried to tell myself that there was no connection between the statue and the dream. I tried to believe I had been working too hard; that I was beginning to imagine things. I thought of a thousand excuses. But I must have known the truth, though I would not admit it even to myself.

The next morning I was up and shaving earlier than I am usually awake. In the mirror I could see the steady dread that showed in my eyes and the dark, sleepless lines rimming my cheekbones. My fingers were trembling when I raised my hand to look at the blue lines etched on the back of it, and when the doorbell rang I jumped and cut myself with the razor.

It was my Uncle Wade.

He stormed in, his white mane of hair blowing back from his forehead, his dark eyes glittering. He waved a newspaper under my face and bellowed, "Look at that! Look, damn it!"

It was a lurid account of the murder, describing the weird atmosphere of the roadhouse and all the gruesome details of the crime. The police claimed that McDavid had been killed by an animal of

some kind, saying that no human being could have torn his throat apart as had been done. The fact that the lights were out at the moment was merely a coincidence, they said, which gave the beast courage to attack. Already a reporter had found two persons who remembered having seen strange animals near the roadhouse. One of them was supposed to have noticed a monstrous dog, while the other said that what he had seen was an ape-like thing.

"Perhaps that's what it was." I almost whispered the words. "Perhaps it was an animal after all, and—"

"What the devil do I care what it was?" Uncle Wade yelled. "These damn newspapers will frighten everybody in the city! There won't be a person in Death's Roadhouse for weeks. If it happened anywhere else it would be a murder and that's all, but with those damn statues . . .!" He began to curse the whole idea and me for having made the models.

"But it was your scheme," I told him, "You asked me to model them."

"I don't give a damn who asked you!" he bellowed. "You made them, and they'll ruin my business." He stormed out of the place, still cursing.

I was supposed to have a date with Neta that afternoon, but I phoned and told her I was feeling ill and would meet her later at the roadhouse. I was afraid to see her, afraid to be alone with her because of the dream crouched like some great cat in the back of my mind, ready to spring.

FOR more than an hour I walked up and down my small apartment, reading the paper Uncle Wade had left. I read the story until I knew it by heart, and gradually the idea that it was a beast which had killed McDavid took root in my mind. "That's what it was," I kept telling myself. "It couldn't have been anything else. In escaping it brushed against me, got blood on me and knocked me unconscious. It was some beast that. . . ." I shuddered, looking down at my hands, with the corded muscles and the queer blue lines on the right one.

Once more I began to think of Tai Ming and the satin smoothness of his voice as he had sworn vengeance. But that was absurd. He couldn't have done this, and anyway he was in China. He had written Neta that he realized we meant no insult. I also thought of Foster Duncan saying, "A Chinaman apologizes for stepping behind you just before he sticks a knife in your back."

About four o'clock I walked down to the corner for the afternoon papers. I wanted to go out, I wanted to quit thinking the terrible thoughts that were gnawing through my brain; and somehow I was almost afraid to leave the apartment. I didn't want to read any more about what had happened last night, and yet I could scarcely wait for the papers to appear on the newsstands.

Seeking a new lead for their stories, the afternoon sheets had played up the wild beast angle. Perhaps the reporters were purposely exaggerating; perhaps hysteria had struck the farmers who lived near Death's Roadhouse. Anyway there were four new reports of persons who had seen some monstrous creature nearby, though none of them had seen it clearly. They told of some great, hairy, ape-like thing which showed for a moment between the trees—and vanished.

It doesn't seem strange now that I felt better when I read of the creature. "Those persons have actually seen it," I thought. "It's the thing that killed John McDavid last night. It's not just the imagination of some frightened persons."

But that night when it was time to go back to the roadhouse, terror returned to me. I could feel it as close to me as the darkness itself, feel it tightening around me, stopping my breath and the very flow of my blood.

If Uncle Wade expected his business to be ruined by the publicity, he was wrong. The place was packed to the walls, though a strange, taut quietness hung over the crowd. Every person there was thinking of last night's tragedy, and they were conscious of the weird influence of the roadhouse. They did not dance close to the wax figures which seemed to writhe under the green lights; and the last tables to fill were those near the statues.

Purposely I avoided Neta. She was sitting at the same table where we had been the night before, and both Foster Duncan and Roger Swanson were with her. I paused once and looked at them, feeling love for the girl rise even with the black terror that surged through me, even with the sudden striking of the dream into my mind—the picture of my hand tearing at her throat. . . .

IT WAS about midnight when Roger Swanson came into the office where I was sitting with Uncle Wade. His thin, handsome face was as sullen as ever beneath his blond curls. "Why are you avoiding Neta?" he asked. "You know she's been trying to speak to you all night."

"I've been busy," I replied. "I haven't had time."

Swanson said, "You're lying. You've been avoiding her, and she knows it."

I don't know what made me lose my temper then. Perhaps the fear had been eating at my brain so long that suddenly it broke through—because for the next few seconds I was a madman. I had my fingers in Swanson's coat and was shaking him, yelling: "Damn it! I'll see her when I want to, and you keep the hell out of it!" I flung him to one side, hurled myself at the door.

16

Behind me Uncle Wade's deep voice was saying, "Well, I'll be—!"

It was that sudden outburst that made me realize how frightened I was. My whole body was trembling, and ice was crushing the breath from my lungs. "I'm going insane," I thought. "Insane with fear of something I don't understand, something that's eating into me. But I can't see it, and I can't touch it."

I stood for a long moment, in the semi-darkness near the wall, and looked at the dance floor. My nails dug into my palms until they brought blood. My whole body was rigid. "I've got to face it," I thought. "I can't hide any longer, or I'll go mad. I've *got* to find out, tonight." My knees were stiff, my body cold as I went toward the table where Neta was sitting with Foster Duncan.

"Hello," Foster said when I came up. "Where have you been all night?"

"Working." I sat down, trying to keep my face blank, to fight down the fear that was like a terrific spring coiled inside me, ready to break loose. But Neta's dark eyes were on mine, and I could feel the worry and the hurt in her gaze. And I felt more than ever my terrific love for her.

"This story about the beast is growing into quite a yarn," Foster remarked. "I've heard several persons claim they saw, or even touched, it—last night. Funny they didn't think to tell the police right after McDavid was killed."

"But it must have been some kind of animal." My voice got suddenly high, shrill. "It *must* have been!"

Foster's dark eyes squinted. "Maybe, maybe not," he said.

A few minutes later Neta got up to sing, and after her act was over, Foster left. When she came back to the table I thought she was going to start asking questions, but she didn't. She just sat there and looked at me with the worry and the hurt showing darkly in her eyes, trying to give me courage by the quiet beauty of her nature. I wanted to tell her what had happened, tell her why I was afraid; yet when I opened my mouth there were no words I could say. It was only a dream and a trick of my imagination which had frightened me, I thought, and to explain that would sound absurd.

But I was afraid to sit here alone with her. I was afraid that looking at her would cause the whole horrific vision to stab like a sword into my brain; that I would start out of my chair, as I had done the night before, lunge toward her, my hands reaching for her throat. And then. . . . So I sat there, my hands gripping the edge of the table, my face turned from hers—though I could feel her eyes watching me.

Whenever I saw acquaintances, I called them over to sit with us, and I talked loudly, nervously. My eyes kept creeping toward the particular statue I had made last night that had changed into an image of myself.

But tonight nothing happened. At about 2:30 most of the crowd began to leave, and at 3:00 the roadhouse was closed.

I knew then what I had to do—because another day of constant dread, of fear ceaselessly gnawing into my mind, would drive me insane. It was the fact that I didn't *know* anything which hurt the most. And I had to know! I had to stay here tonight alone. I had to find out!

NETA, Roger Swanson, Uncle Wade and I gathered in the parking lot after the roadhouse was closed. "Damn bunch of morbid-minded thrill searchers," Uncle Wade yelled. "They'll storm the place for a night or two and then when nothing happens they'll all quit coming."

"They haven't quit coming yet," Swanson said. "I'm getting you fifty thousand dollars worth of free advertising out of this."

"Damn you and your advertising! Damn Jim and his wax models! A man would be better born without a family." Uncle Wade crawled into his automobile, slammed the door. I saw his white hair gleam in the dashlight. Then his car tore out of the lot.

I turned to Neta. "I've got to stay and do a little work. Roger will drive you home, and I'll see you in the morning."

She faced me squarely, her face tilted up to look into mine, her dark eyes defiant. "I'm not sleepy," she said flatly. "I'll stay until you finish your work."

I tried to argue with her. I even lost my temper and screamed that I didn't want her, but she only stood there straight and slim. "I'm staying," she said.

Swanson said, "I'll be glad to drive you home, but you'll have to come along now. I'm not going to stand here all night and listen to a lover's quarrel."

Neta said, "I'll wait for Jim." She turned and went toward the dark roadhouse.

"Well, that's that." Swanson kicked his motor into action, swung his car out of the parking lot.

Neta was leaning against the door when I reached her. I opened the door with my key, reached through and switched on the light. Without speaking I went down the corridor which led to the large dining room. My fingers fumbled along the wall, found the switch, and the wavering green light smeared out over the empty dance floor, the deserted tables, and over the ghastly wax statues which seemed to tremble and pulse with the eerie light.

I stood there, motionless, while the weird spell of the place began to tighten about me. My eyes strained against the semi-gloom as I sought the statue—which

last night had pictured my hands ripping the throat of John McDavid.

Neta's fingers tightened on my arm, pulled me around to face her. In the green light her skin took on a horrible corpse-like appearance. Fear showed plainly in her dark eyes, but her chin was firm. "All right," she said. "Now tell me what's happened. What's made you act this way? Why did you look like you did, just before McDavid was killed last night?"

I didn't answer. I just stood there staring at her, feeling an agony of cold terror crush in against my ribs.

"What is it?" she asked again. "Tell me."

What could I say? I couldn't tell her the truth. I didn't know what the truth was. I loved Neta with every muscle and fibre in me; I didn't want her to believe me insane. Looking at her I could feel the dream gathering furiously in my mind, swelling like a great spring that must snap free at any moment. What if it came again while we were here alone? What if I saw a vision of my hand at her throat?

"Get out of here," I screamed. "Take my car and drive to the city. Get out, damn it!"

She recoiled a half-step, and I saw her eyes widen and her mouth jerk. Then she was close to me again, her hands on my chest. "You've got to tell me what's wrong, Jim. I love you."

"Listen," I said. "I want you to go home. I've got an idea about what killed McDavid last night, and I want to investigate it. It won't be safe for you here."

"You mean you saw—somebody?"

"No. I don't know what it was. But I want to find out and you—"

"I'm staying," she cut in. "It's as safe for me as it is for you. If it's what the papers say—some kind of a beast—it may be miles away from here by now." There was a strange light in her eyes as she looked at me. I couldn't tell how much she believed. But I knew that she loved me, and though she was small and quiet and modest there was an indomitable courage inside her.

"I'm going to look at the statues." I turned on my heel and began to walk around the room, pausing at each wax image, thumping it with my fingers to make sure it was exactly as I had originally made it.

I was half-way around when it happened.

Neta's voice called out suddenly, sharp with terror, "Jim, what—!"

I spun to face her.

SHE was near the edge of the dance floor. Just in front of her were wax figures representing Peter Caroway, the man who murdered four wives by slashing their throats with a razor, and one of the women he had killed. In eerie, moving light it seemed that the blood was seeping down the woman's throat. Beyond Neta was the model of a man splitting a woman's head with a hatchet, and close behind her was a huge wax Chinese, his long finger nails glittering in the light, his hands almost circling Neta's throat.

"What is it?" I called to her. "What's happened?"

Slowly her face lost its expression of terror, but when she smiled her lips were still quivering. "Nothing. I thought I heard somebody. It's just that this place has got on my nerves."

"It would—" I started to say it would get on anybody's nerves, but I never finished. I began to lean forward, body stiff, eyes bulging. There was something about the wax face of the Chinese, the color it took as the lights flickered over it, and the eyes which seemed to be glaring down at Neta.

"Good God," I whispered. I couldn't

say any more. My breath was like jagged ice in my throat and nostrils, and my lips were suddenly stiff with terror. *For the Chinese bending above Neta had the eyes and mouth of Tai Ming!* The whole face had a terrible, horrific resemblance to that of the man who had sworn revenge. It was contorted with unbelievable savageness. It was old without showing age, like the face of a demon who has lived through eternity.

And in that same terrifying instant I knew that I had never made this statue!

I don't know what made Neta take that half-step backward. Perhaps it was the look on my face from which she recoiled instinctively. Perhaps she cried out. But I heard no sound, because the very air of the room seemed to have congealed about me, holding me cold and utterly still. I only know that she did step backward so that her throat was within an inch of the Chinese's hands—and it was in that instant that I knew he was not a wax figure!

I saw the light gleam on his fingernails as they moved. I saw his eyes widen and the savage light in them leap like a flame. I tried to scream at Neta, tried to hurl my body in a mad rush toward her, but I made no sound and I did not move. It was as if I had become one of my own statues, though inside me terror was a black cyclone bursting against my ribs.

The light glittered like green flame along the Chinese's finger nails again—and they were at Neta's throat.

I moved then. It was a sudden leap, as if the spring of terror, which had been coiling in me for two days, had abruptly snapped. I heard the loud, jangling scream that slashed the air, the machine-gun beat of my shoes. I was racing toward her across the dance floor, arms flailing, a man gone mad with terror.

I think she screamed too. She half spun, her hands coming up in front of her breasts, then lunged backward to strike against the pedestal on which the Chinese stood. Together they went over, with a crash.

I tried to swerve and stop running, but I was going too hard. My right foot hit the overturned pedestal, and suddenly I was in the air, seeming to hang there like a feather. Then the dance floor tilted upward and I struck it, hard. The green lights flickered into a black, quivering darkness through which I tried time and again to fight my way back to consciousness.

I couldn't have been stunned for more than ten seconds. I could feel Neta's hands on my shoulders and hear her voice, before I could see her, saying: "Jim, Jim, what is it?" Then I was on my feet stumbling toward the overturned pedestal and the still figure of the Chinese beyond it. He was lying face downward, bent from the waist, his claw-like hands holding his body from the floor.

I caught him by the shoulders and jerked with all my strength. "Damn you!" I yelled. "I—"

It was a figure of wax, one I had fashioned with my own hands, not a month before. And staring into its face I could see absolutely no resemblance to Tai Ming!

CHAPTER THREE

Blood—and the Symbol Again!

HOW long I stood there without moving I don't know. My eyes had swollen until they ached against the sockets. My mouth was open, but there was no air in my lungs, and a cord of ice was cutting into my ribs. Perhaps it was only my imagination, I thought. Perhaps the figure had never had any resemblance to Tai Ming. The flickering lights might have made it seem to move, reflected in its glass eyes—and I might have imagined the fury and murder which I saw there. But if all this were imagination, then. . . .

There was only one answer. I was going insane.

But insanity couldn't have put those lines on my right hand. They were tangible evidence I actually had. Suddenly I was glad because of them—and I raised my right hand, tilting my eyes downward to find the blue lines. I wanted to see them, make sure they were really there.

Abruptly, Neta screamed!

The cry shot high and terrible, jerking at my fear-cold muscles, turning them slowly. I was half-way around when a man's voice said: "Hell! There's more yelling going on here this time of morning, than there is while the place is running."

At the far edge of the dance floor, barely visible through the dim light a man was standing. Even in the semi-darkness I could see the high, sharp angles of his face, the arched brows and the way his eyes glittered in the flickering lights. His whole face was Satanic, and his mouth curled with the savage humor of the Devil.

Neta cowered against me. Her hands were tugging at my arms, and she was making small whimpering sounds, deep in her throat. But courage began to come back to me. Here, at last, was something definite, something I would put my hands on and fight.

"Who the hell are you?" I called out.

He crossed the dance floor with a lanky, loose jointed stride. The smile on his face was confident, disdainful. "I go by the plain name of Bill Jones," he said. "You can believe it or not, but it's true. And like a good newspaper reporter I already know who you are, and don't need to ask."

I recognized him now from pictures I

20

had seen in the *Times Democrat*. He was a man in his early thirties, but fast gaining a national reputation. Only a few months before, he had published a book of savagely humorous essays, and a year ago he had won the Pulitzer Prize for reporting.

"What was that big crash I heard?" he asked. "Did you find the ape, or the werewolf—or any of the other things persons have been seeing since last night?"

"No. I just stumbled over one of the statues and upset it." I could feel Neta's eyes on me, could feel the terror and the question in them, but I wouldn't look at her.

"What are you doing here this time of night?" Jones asked. "You got any idea about the killing?"

For a moment I looked at him. He was lank but there was an indication of strength in his tall body, and his face was completely without fear. It would be good to have him with us, I thought. If the stories of the beast were true and we found the thing, he could help with the fight which would follow. If it were not a beast which had killed McDavid. . . . The dream, crouched in the black portions of my mind, was constantly gathering strength, growing larger and larger. If it struck suddenly, then Jones would be there to protect Neta.

"I had an idea about that killing, and I stayed to investigate," I replied. "Miss Phillips stayed with me, though I tried to get her to go home."

There was a sudden tightening of his gaunt body. The angles of his face seemed to grow more sharp, his dark eyes glittered. "Yes?" he said.

"It's about the statues," I explained. "Last night, just before McDavid was killed, I thought I saw a statue which I hadn't made. I was too far away to be certain and, before I could investigate, the lights went out."

He grinned. "I'd been wondering about these statues. That's one reason I came out tonight. Let's get started."

WE DIDN'T find anything after going over the entire room carefully, tapping on every statue, making absolutely certain that they were the same wax figures I had modeled. And all the while fear crawled like some horrible worm inside me, eating its way toward my brain. Somehow I knew that we would not find the figures which I had seen, and I tried to make myself believe that there were no such figures—except in my half crazed imagination.

But I kept telling myself that those statues had to exist; and I thought of the beast which persons claimed to have seen. What if we found it—a thing which could rip open a throat and vanish again during a few moment of darkness? I wanted to keep Neta close to me, with my arm around her, and protect her with my body. . . . And I was afraid of the dream lurking like a storm inside me, afraid of the picture in the back of my mind, of my own bloody hands at Neta's torn throat.

"Well," Jones said, when we had finished searching the dining room, "is that all?"

"There are a few in the attic," I answered. "I've been using it for a studio, but there are no lights up there."

Jones shrugged. "There should be candles—somewhere."

We found some in the kitchen, and he and I each took one. "Come on," he said. "How do we get up there?"

The stairway winds up from the back hallway. The steps haven't been painted in years and are soft with decay, so that our shoes made dull, hollow sounds as we went up them. I led, Neta followed, and Jones came last. The light of the candles flickered like a yellow wave over the narrow walls, licked into the blackness in front of me, and faded.

I reached the top and stopped until they came abreast of me. The candle light flickered out across the floor, touched on the ghastly face of a statue lying on its back, and oozed into darkness beyond. Through the great sky-light overhead I could see tiny, white stars deep sunken in a black sky.

Jones took a half-step forward, swinging his candle so that the light rippled out into the darkness. For an instant a beastial face, long lips snarled back from yellow teeth, an up-raised hand clutching a gleaming knife-blade, were visible. Neta made a choked cry and flung herself against me.

"It's one of my statues," I said. "I haven't finished it yet."

Jones swung the candle back so that the light fell on the wax figure again. "Very neat," he said. "This whole place would fit in with a good bloody murder."

I didn't answer him. Perhaps I already knew what was coming, or maybe the strain was beginning to tell, for my nerves were drawn to the cracking point. But certainly fear was in me as it had never been before, starting deep in my stomach, storming upward. And with it the dream was crowding closer against my brain.

I said, "Stay here, Neta, with him. I want to look around." I moved ahead, the candle light wavering ahead of me and shimmering over the wax figure stretched on the floor. I stooped beside it, ran my hand over its cold, contorted face. I knew that it was wax, and I knew that I had made it, but I wanted to spend as much time as possible before I moved farther into the darkness.

I felt that there was something gruesome and horrible beyond bearing hidden in that black sea; and I wanted to avoid it. I wanted to leap to my feet and run

screaming from the attic, go plunging down the rotting stairs, away from Death's Roadhouse, to find bright lights and crowds. But somehow I fought my muscles to steadiness and stood up, facing into the darkness beyond the candle light. It was there and I knew it, crouched like a black panther, waiting for me. My mind was already tottering on the edge of insanity, but I had to face this thing and find out what it was.

I stepped forward, and the light flowed ahead while darkness closed in thickly behind me. At that moment there was not even the sound of breathing—nothing except the dull thud of my steps. One, two, three, I took. . . .

Then I smelled the thing which was something of an odor, but more the feeling of ancient Chinese walls, heavy with history!

I knew it was going to happen. I knew that I couldn't stop it; it was too late to run now, too late even to scream out to warn Neta. I was like a man in a dream who sees himself walking toward death and is unable to stop; like a bird looking into a snake's eyes, seeing the snake come toward him and unable even to flutter his wings.

I don't know how I raised the candle and held it farther in front of me. Perhaps I didn't really move at all, and it was only the light which stretched into the darkness, to touch faintly on the waxen image. The thing was almost completely hidden in darkness and I never saw it clearly, but in that first shuddering instant I knew what it was. It was a statue of myself holding a man with my left arm while my right hand ripped out windpipe and jugular vein. And the man I held was the reporter, Bill Jones!

For a second that hung poised and, separated from all time, I stood there.

22

Then, inside me, the cyclone of terror and madness burst.

I can still hear in my mind's sound-memory the scream that shot upward and reverberated under the vaulted walls of the attic; that slashed and beat at the darkness. I recall the candle falling from my hand as I turned, and the way its flame sputtered and went out as it fell. I remember the yellow circle of light that Jones' candle made and my body hurdling through the blackness toward it, but I don't think I ever saw the reporter's face. Headlong I struck him, and we were both crashing over and his candle was out, so that darkness seemed almost to hurtle through the huge attic. . . .

I fought something that fought with me. My hands were deep-buried in a part of it, jerking and tearing. Then, slowly, the darkness oozed into my mind, and there was no sensation or memory left.

I WAS on my knees and had been there a long time, it seemed. The darkness was like a wet blanket held flat against my eyes. There was no sound except the dull beat of my heart, the whisper of air through my open mouth. I blinked hard at the darkness, strained my eyelids wide open, in an effort to see. I slid my right hand across the floor in front of me— and then I touched it!

In that first instant I knew what it was. I felt the blood damp on my palm, oozing between my fingers, and I felt the flesh that was still warm and horribly slimey. It was a human body, with its throat torn wide-open!

Somehow I kept from screaming. Perhaps I couldn't have screamed, for at first I was numb, and there was no thought, no emotion in my brain. Then memory crawled back into my brain and I recalled the statue and the struggle on the floor

and the screams that had beat like furious wings in the darkness.

Then I heard the sounds, like claws slowly raking the floor, and a husky, labored breathing. And into my mind crashed the picture of the ape-thing, which persons claimed to have seen.

I was lost in the pitch blackness of the attic with the thing which ripped the throats from its victims!

I tried to stop breathing then, to still the very beating of my heart, for fear the sound would give me away. I had no idea where I was in the attic, or in which direction I faced. I was afraid to move, afraid to make any attempt to escape, lest the floor creak under me.

And then another thought began to form in my brain. What had happened to Neta? Was she alive in the attic? Had she escaped, or—Good God! Suppose the torn throat I had touched, the blood that smeared my hand, were hers!

I think I stopped breathing. Every muscle in my body began to contract upon itself, while there was a lump in my throat that was like fingers digging at my own windpipe. Somehow I started my right hand across the floor toward the body which I knew was there, although I could not see it. The blood smeared out under my fingers as they moved.

It was that oozing blood which brought full consciousness and realization bursting into my mind. My hand was thick with blood, and I could feel it congealing over my wrist and forearm. It was impossible to have got that much on me from merely touching the body! How had the blood got there?

There was only one answer—and I fought it with every fibre of my brain. I hadn't killed the reporter! I *couldn't* have! I had heard a sound in the darkness that must be the beast. It had to be —because if there were no beast, then I. . . . And if there *was* a beast here in the darkness, then what had happened to Neta?

I wanted to call her, to hear her voice so that I would know she was alive. But what if she didn't answer, if the figure blotted out by the darkness was hers? And if she did answer and the beast were in the room, what would happen then? Again I thought of my hands and the sticky blood smeared over them, and in my mind there was a picture of the statue I had seen; a vision of myself ripping the throat from Bill Jones.

How long I crouched there staring into the darkness I don't know. Abruptly I heard the sound again, a claw scratching on the dank flooring. I couldn't stand it any longer then. I had to know!

Suddenly my voice was screaming into the darkness, shouting with wild, maniacal fury: "Neta, Neta, where are you, what's happened?" My left hand plunged into my coat pocket, came out with a match. Even as the yellow flame spurted I heard Neta's short cry, the frantic tap of her heels on the floor. All at once, she was in my arms, sobbing.

I remember the moments that followed only as a horrible agony through which I went, knowing already what had happened. I found the candle, lit it, and gazed down at the mutilated body of Bill Jones, at the black pool of blood under his torn throat. I circled the attic, praying to find some beast that could have killed him, praying that it would attack me—and knowing all the time that no such thing existed. I looked at every wax figure in the place, but there was none I hadn't sculptured. The statues with my face and face of Bill Jones did not exist.

Finally I turned to look at Neta; and in her eyes knowledge was a quivering and horrible certainty. She backed away from me, cringing.

I couldn't let her look at me that way.

"Neta," I whispered, "don't look at me like that. I didn't kill—" I reached out toward her, the candle light flickering brightly across my bloody hands.

I think she screamed then and leaped from me. But I had ceased to notice her. I could feel my eyelids stretching wide, eyes bulging as I looked at the back of my hand.

Beneath the congealing blood, the blue lines had become viciously clear as though they were etched there with blue flame. *There was no doubting now that it was some kind of Chinese symbol!*

CHAPTER FOUR

The Vengeance of the Gods

A GREEN shaded light threw a bright cone of illumination over the desk and the square-faced police sergeant seated behind it. Neta was in a chair to the left, her face strangely pale in contrast to her black hair. In the semi-darkness behind me I could feel the eyes of the detectives who stood watching, near the wall.

"All right," the sergeant said. His voice was low and brittle, his eyes as lusterless as buttons as he looked into mine. "Let's hear your story again, and make sure you are telling the truth."

I leaned forward, put both hands on the edge of his desk. When I did the blue Chinese lines gleamed on the back of my right hand. I clenched it suddenly, thrust it deep into my pocket, shuddering. "I've told you what happened," I said. "Why do I have to go through it again?"

Neta leaned forward, deathly pale. For a moment I thought she would faint, but she steadied herself. "Please, Sergeant, we are so tired. Can't you let us go now? We've told you everything."

The sergeant turned his black eyes on her. In the back of the room I heard the restless movement of a detective's foot, heard one of them whispering to another.

The sergeant said, "I'll let you go very soon, miss. I want to hear Mr. Farlan's story again just to get it straight." His eyes came back to me, dull, expressionless and yet seeming to reach through my eyes to the very terror that was in me. "All right," he said, "let's hear it."

I told him about meeting Bill Jones while we were searching the roadhouse, but I did not tell him of the statue which I had seen come to life. "We went into the attic," I told him, "Jones and I carrying candles. It's dark there. You saw how dark it was. I stepped away from Jones and Miss Phillips and then I—I saw something and—"

"You saw *what?*" The detective's voice was never loud but it was hard and brittle as pig-iron.

"I—" My voice began to get hysterical. My hands were gripping the edge of the desk again, shaking it. "I—I don't know what it was! It was in the dark and I just—"

"What did it look like? If you saw it you've got to have some idea."

"I tell you I don't know," I yelled. "Perhaps it wasn't anything—and I just imagined it. Perhaps it was a statue, and because of the candle light I thought it moved. But it—it—" I knew I had to tell them something—anything but the truth. "It looked big and black, and shapeless, but I thought it had eyes. It frightened me. I staggered back against Jones, and both our candles went out. Then something struck me—and I don't remember what happened after that. When I came to Miss Phillips, and—the reporter and I were there—alone. That's when we telephoned to you."

"There's blood on your coat," the sergeant said, utterly without expression. "And there was a little on your wrist, though your hands were very clean, when we reached there."

I could feel Neta's eyes on me, and the eyes of all the detectives hidden in the semi-darkness of the room. Across the desk the sergeant sat, quiet and blank-faced as a graven image. But the very dullness of his gaze set new terror grasping at my throat.

"I know," I had to swallow before I could make the words coherent. "In the dark I touched Jones and got his blood on me. I couldn't stand it—and I washed my hands before you came."

For a minute that dragged into years, the sergeant watched me. Then he said, "And what are those funny blue lines on the back of your hand? The ones that look like a Chinese laundry mark?"

I couldn't keep the fear out of my eyes then, and my mouth began to jerk. "I don't know what they are. They have been on there for a week or more."

IT WAS an hour later that they let us go. If it hadn't been for Neta they might have held me, though there was very little evidence. But Neta corroborated my story on every statement, and though I could feel the horror and the dread in her eyes when she looked at me, she never mentioned my wild charge at the Chinese statue or the way I had whirled and leaped into Bill Jones. But when we came out of the police station into the early morning sunlight, she said, avoiding my gaze: "I'll take a cab and go home. It's out of your way; you don't need to drive me." There was a taut, trembling sound to her voice.

"But I want to take you home. It's no trouble and—" I stopped, seeing the wild dread in her face, the way she instinctively cringed from me. And there was love in her eyes, too, a love that struggled against the horror inside her.

My voice was a dead pain in my throat when I said, "All right, I'll call a cab for you." One was passing and I hailed it, stood flatfooted on the curb watching as she got in and rode off.

It was when I turned toward my own car that I saw the police sergeant standing in the doorway, watching me. His face was as expressionless as ever, his eyes lusterless as buttons. I almost ran toward my car then, and my hands were shaking so that the gears clashed badly when I started.

It was almost two full days since I had been asleep. Yet I paced nervously up and down for hours after reaching my apartment. Time and again I would throw myself on the bed and lie there, face buried in the pillow, hands gripping the cover, trembling. But even then I kept my eyes open. I was afraid, if I shut them, that a black flood of sleep would come over me. . . .

IT WAS about noon when Foster Duncan came in. His gaunt, dark face looked more hollow than ever, more strangely in contrast to the odd sense of humor which always marked his conversation. Fear showed plainly in his sunken eyes.

"I read in the afternoon papers about what happened," he said. "I came right on over here to talk to you." He dropped into a chair, dug out a cigarette. When he lit it, I saw that his fingers were trembling.

"Listen," he said, "what do you make of all this? Have you any ideas about it?"

I turned toward him slowly. "What do you mean?"

For a moment he puffed on his cigarette, then flicked off the ash. "I know it sounds crazy, but I've been thinking about this thing, and I can't get over the idea that Tai Ming is behind it. He swore to have revenge on us. You drew the pictures, and you'd be the one he'd start on. The other night we were talking about him, and you looked so damned odd just before the lights went out and McDavid got killed. And then last night. . . . Even from the newspaper story I could tell that the police suspect you. This morning I got one of these break-my-back-bowing-to-be-polite-letters from Tai. He was too doggone apologetic about having lost his temper with us. A Chink will brush your clothes with a whiskbroom so that when he stabs you in the back he won't get his knife dirty. And then that funny looking Chinese thing on the back of your hand. Where did it come from?"

Instinctively I jerked backward, and my hand came up rigidly before my face. "What—! How did you know about that?"

"I can see it on your hand now, and I saw it last night, and night before last, just after McDavid was killed. It was never there before. What caused it?"

"I—I don't know." I stared at the thing without breathing, without seeing it almost, though every tiny part of it was etched indelibly in my mind. Somehow it began to take on a new and terrible fascination as I looked, and in my mind the low, silky voice of Tai Ming swearing revenge sounded again. But Tai was in China now. How could he have anything to do with the horrors taking place thousands of miles away from him? He had written Neta and Foster that he no longer held any grudge. But why hadn't he written me?

After Foster had gone I sat for more than an hour staring blankly at the lines on the back of my hand. Where had they come from? Perhaps it was only a bruise, and its curious Chinese shape was only a coincidence. But I couldn't make myself believe that, and the longer I looked at it the more convinced I became that it had some secret meaning, some wierd and hòrrific significance.

"I've got to know," I said aloud. "It doesn't really mean anything, but I've got to know."

I WAS halfway to the door before I began to wonder whom I could ask. I only knew one Chinese in the city personally, a young man taking his doctor's degree at the university, but I didn't want to ask him. Suppose these marks did have some meaning? Suppose they told the story of what had happened these past two nights at Death's Roadhouse? Would Lee Sung go to the police and tell them what he had read on the back of my hand? I didn't know, but I didn't want to take the chance. "It will be better to ask someone who doesn't know me," I thought.

I left my automobile and took a street car to China Town. At the first Chinese restaurant I passed I got off the car and went in. It was a small dark place, heavy with the odor of food. A waiter, seated at a small table in the back, was talking with two other Chinese. The shrill babble of their voices sounded eerie and strange in the semi-darkness.

I went straight up to them, moving stiff-kneed, face rigid. "Do any of you speak English?"

They all three stood up. "Yes," two of them began at once, "speak vellee well!"

"All right," I said. "Can any of you tell me what this means?" I pulled my right hand from my pocket, held it palm-down before them. In the dim light the blue lines were dully visible.

Two of the men looked at it blankly, then at me, shaking their heads. But all at once the third man was taut, rigid, bending over my hand, his own yellow fingers coming upward, quivering. Then he was backing away from me, shrilling

terrified words in Chinese. The other two swung toward him for one half instant, and the yellow masks of their faces broke into trembling horror. They backed away from me, half crouching, toward the rear of the restaurant.

For a long moment I stared after them, looking from one face to another. Then terror seized me. "What is it?" I yelled. "What does it mean?" I started forward, hands raised to shake the truth from them.

The waiter screamed, an unbelievably high, piercing shriek. Then, like a trained dance chorus, all three turned and leaped for the door. For a moment they blocked the portal, pawing, jibbering at one another—and were gone.

I FOUND Lee Sung in his apartment on Greensboro Avenue. He is a small man from the south of China with the bland imperturbable face, the polished manners of the well-bred Oriental. "What is it?" he asked me in English that held no trace of accent. "You look worried."

"I am." I lighted a cigarette and began to smoke nervously. He watched me with dark, unfathomable eyes.

"Several days ago," I said slowly, "some lines began to show up on the back of my right hand. They looked like a Chinese letter, and I didn't know where they came from. I don't mean to trouble you, but I was down in Chinatown today for lunch, and some Chinese saw the lines and jumped up and ran away. That got me interested. I showed the waiter my hand. He ran, too. I was frightened, and wanted to know. . . ."

His expression never changed. "Perhaps I can tell you. Let me see."

I put out my right hand and caught the arm of his chair. Through an open window, afternoon sunlight fluttered in a golden stream over my sunburned skin, making the blue lines come brilliantly

27

alive. Lee Sung leaned over and peered at them.

There was no perceptible change in his face. Suddenly, however, it was stiff and mask-like, and his expression might have been modeled in wax. After a moment he raised his slant eyes to mine.

"Well?" I said huskily.

"This is going to sound strange to you because you are not acquainted with Chinese customs and beliefs. Not all of us believe it ourselves. It is what you refer to as a superstition in English. And yet it is so well-founded—it has been confirmed by history so often—that it is impossible for the most educated of us to disbelieve entirely."

"What are you trying to tell me?" My voice was tense, edged with hysteria.

"You are acquainted with the ancient Roman custom of household gods, minor deities who look after the welfare and the safety of the home. The Chinese household gods are not so well known, perhaps because they differ in one major respect from those of the Romans, whose gods were dieties who protected the home by keeping the fires burning, the members of the family healthy and other similar services. The Chinese gods do not protect the home. They are jealous, demonlike creatures who revenge insults to the family honor. Sometimes they are represented as a kind of half beast and half man, sometimes as the most powerful and blood-thirsty of the family's ancestors. But always they are terrible supernatural creatures who exist only to destroy those who have insulted the family they protect."

I was half out of my chair now, fingers digging into its arms, my weight resting on the balls of my feet, body drawn taut. "And this—this mark on my arm?"

Lee Sung said, "That is the seal by which one of these demons would mark his victim."

I slumped back into my chair, limp and not even trembling. In that first moment I accepted without reservation what he had said. At first my mind did not even struggle for hope and I *knew* the truth —that there was no escape.

But a man cannot cease to hope and to fight for existence very long. I was standing up pacing the floor, my hands clenching and unclenching nervously. "But that's absurd," I said. "You know such things can't exist. That's an old folk-tale."

"Yes?" He said the one word flatly.

I whirled on him. "*You* don't believe it! You can't believe that sort of thing!"

He made a gesture with his fragile, yellow fingers. "No. I don't believe it. And I don't disbelieve it. I have seen this mark before and...." He gestured with his thin hands again. "I don't want to see it on me. Probably I would commit suicide."

"No!" I hurled the word at him. "Why would you do that? How do these demons revenge themselves?"

"There are many ways. Their victims have been found frozen in the ice of rivers. They have been driven mad. They have died of disease—some very bad disease."

I don't remember leaving Lee Sung's apartment. I don't remember the next few hours. I only know that it was twilight when I came, and that there was one thing in my mind, dominating every thought and action, driving me like a whip-lash. I had to get away. I had to escape. During those hours of blankness the dream had moved into the front of my brain, and there was never a moment now when I was not conscious of it. At every step I took the picture of Neta, her head thrown back across my left arm, her throat torn and bloody, moved before me. I had to get away before I saw her again.

Instinctively, terribly, I knew that the next time it would be Neta who was killed.

I was going up the steps of my apartment when I saw the man standing on the sidewalk about forty yards away. For a half instant I paused, looking at him. And then, sick at heart, I crossed the porch, pulled open the door and went into the house. For I had seen that same man several times today without paying any attention to him, but now I knew who he was—a detective! As long as he watched me, there would be no chance to escape.

I didn't give up hope of getting away. I took all the money that was in my apartment, dropped a few small valuables into my pockets, and slipped out the back door. I had gone a block and a half when I saw the other man following me. I knew that he, too, was a detective. I stopped in the drug store, bought another pack of cigarettes and went back to my place. I tried once more, just after dark fell, but it was no use. I couldn't slip away from them.

It was then that I decided to go to Death's Roadhouse. I knew that if the detective became too suspicious about me, I would be carried to police headquarters for questioning. Somehow I couldn't face the sergeant's eyes again.

ALMOST everyone knows what happened at the roadhouse that night. Papers from one end of the country to the other made big stories of it. But I am the only one who knows why it happened, although the whole country wondered, and, during my trial, the court made an effort to force me to confess. I didn't want to tell, and I refused. But after I'm electrocuted, Friday night, I

want Neta to know. That is one reason I'm writing this.

I kept away from Neta all the early part of that night. I wouldn't even go near the table where we generally sat. Whenever I saw Roger or Foster Duncan coming toward me, I ran from them. Once I met Neta's gaze full on me, but she did not call and I turned quickly away.

It happened shortly after midnight.

I was seated across the room from Neta, drinking heavily; but the liquor hadn't seemed to have any effect on me. I was so nervous that twice my drinks sloshed over as I raised the glass to my mouth.

From where I sat I could see Neta at a table with Roger and Uncle Wade, but I tried to keep from looking at her. I don't know what force it was that turned my eyes toward her time and again. I could see only her profile, a gruesome, greenish shade under the flickering lights. She was wearing her black hair differently tonight, combed back from her forehead and fluffy and loose around her neck. It was like this that I had seen her in the dream. Every time that I glanced at her, now, the vision came storming back into my mind with a new and mounting horror.

"It's going to happen tonight," I thought. "It will happen tonight and I can't stop it. I can't even run from it, because it has already reached across thousands of miles and there is no avoiding it." I shook myself the way a dog shakes water from his coat, and I gripped the edge of the table until my nails and knuckles were a sickly white.

"I won't really hurt Neta," I promised myself. "I couldn't hurt her because I love her more than I do my own life. I *couldn't* hurt her." Yet I knew even then that it was coming.

I asked the waiter to bring me another

drink, waving at him furiously with my whole arm. "Listen," I told him, "I want a bottle of Scotch, and I want it quickly. You don't need to worry about the soda."

He looked at me curiously. "You are doing a lot of drinking tonight, Mr. Farlan. Do you think—?"

"Damn it," I yelled at him, "bring me the bottle. I don't need to think."

"Yes sir," he said, and turned away.

But the liquor did no good. It didn't dull the terror that was gathering inside my chest, and it didn't wipe out the vision of Neta's torn throat. Instead it seemed that with every swallow I took, the knowledge came clearer and clearer inside me. "It's going to happen tonight," I whispered aloud. "I can't stop it." I glanced toward Neta. Her face was almost lurid under the green wavering lights. Almost viciously I jerked my gaze away.

And then I saw it!

In the dull shadows near the wall not twenty feet from me, was a statue identically like the others. But this time it was Neta's contorted face which stared up into mine—and from her throat the blood gushed horribly.

I don't recall getting to my feet. I heard the crash of the whiskey bottle and then the heavier boom of the overturned table. There was a startled cry from persons near me, then abrupt silence crashing through the crowded roadhouse. Somehow I was walking toward the statue, wavering from side to side, my big hands claw-like in front of me. Even as the darkness started sliding into my brain, I knew that I was not going toward the statue at all—but toward Neta!

The vision of her torn throat and spilling blood burst like a shell under my skull. At the same instant from deep inside me there came the choked scream of my emotions, saying: "You love her. You love her more than your own life.

You can't hurt her." I heard my own voice shouting insanely over and over: "I killed them. I killed them—and I'll kill her. You've got to stop me."

There were hands on me, hurling me down and I got one brief glimpse of the detective's face. After that there was nothing, not even memory.

AND NOW, so help me God, I have written the entire truth as I know it. The detectives caught me before I could reach Neta. They used my shouted confession to convict me of the other two murders. At the trial, I asked for no defense because I wanted none. I wanted to be locked in this small death cell from which there is no escaping, except down the short corridor which leads into eternity.

And here, back of these barred windows through which even the sunlight comes dimly, I am still afraid that if I were released the thing would happen again. This time they might not be able to save Neta. It is better that I should die, and I am glad that it is only a short while now before they come for me.

* * *

WHEN I stipulated that this account should not be read until after my execution I didn't realize the horrible consequence which might result. I believed that I would be in the death cell, alone, until the guards came for me; that it would be impossible for me to do any harm. I had told the prison authorities that I wanted no visitors. It didn't seem possible to me that I would ever again come face to face with Neta Phillips.

She must have exerted a great deal of political pull or even bribery to reach me. It was late at night and the curious, death-like silence that hangs over prisons had stilled the very air in my cell.

Through the barred door a dim grey light spilled, leaving the corners of the cell and the steel bunk in deep shadows. I sat on the bunk, shoulders hunched, and stared at the black bars of the window against a blue-black sky.

There was the hushed whisper of a guard's shoes in the corridor, the louder *tap-tap* of other steps. I didn't even turn. Perhaps it is only now that I realize that I heard those steps, for I was never aware of the door opening, or of the sound of it closing again. I just sat there, shoulders hunched, my mind as blank as the window at which I stared.

"Jim," Neta's voice was very soft, and I thought at first that I was dreaming. Then she said, "Jim!" again, and all at once I was on my feet, spinning to face her.

She and Roger Swanson stood just inside the barred door. Her slim figure showed plainly against the lighted corridor, but her face was in the shadows. I saw her hands, like small white birds as she raised them to reach for me. "Darling," she said, "I've wanted to see you for so long. I had to come." She stepped toward me.

With one great leap I went backward and struck against the far wall of the cell. "Keep away from me," I shouted. "Don't come any closer."

She paused, one foot still in front of the other, her hands raised. "Jim!" There was a terrible hurt in her voice. "What have I done? Why did you avoid me all during the trial? Why are you acting like this?" Her words were very low, as though the deep silence of the prison had affected her so that she whispered unconsciously. During all the time that she was there none of us spoke loudly. Even when I shouted at her the sound was scarcely above a hoarse whisper.

I had to swallow the terror mounting in my throat before I could answer her

question. "It's nothing you've done. It's me. I've gone insane. You've got to keep away from me or—or—" I couldn't say she would be murdered as the men had been. I couldn't force the words out of my throat.

In the utter stillness of the cell I could hear her breathing as she looked at me, silent, pleading with her eyes. Roger Swanson was standing near the door watching us quietly. "You're not insane," Neta said finally. "But you're in some kind of trouble. You've got to tell me what it is. Perhaps I can help you. If you had let me see you during the trial—"

"I don't want to see you." I hurled the words at her in that queer whispered scream which the prison had forced on me. "I told them not to let you in here. And I wish to God you'd get out while there's time. I don't ever want to see you again."

She made a choked, gasping cry and stepped backwards. Then all at once she had slumped on the bunk and terrible, racked sobs shook her body.

"God, I can't stand this," Roger Swanson said hoarsely. He pulled a flask from his pocket, unscrewed the top with one twist and raised it to his lips.

With two long strides I passed Neta and reached him, snatched the flask from his hands. "I need it!" I turned it up and gulped at it until it was dry, then handed it back to him. In all the prison there was no sound except Neta's racked sobbing and the rasping of my own breath.

Abruptly I swung toward her. "Get out," I said softly. "Please get out, quickly. You've got to go, because soon. . . ."

I was still speaking when I smelled that odor which was not an odor at all, but rather the feeling of ancient Chinese walls. And in that instant I knew what was coming.

"Oh God!" I tried to cry aloud, but

the words choked in my throat. I tried to scream at her, to scream for the guards to come and hold me. My mouth jerked with the terrible and searing effort to cry out, but there was no sound.

I was wavering toward her and though I tried to stop myself I could not. It was as if I were off balance, and instinctively I stumbled forward to keep from falling. I could feel my hands coming up, the big fingers hooked, claw-like, reaching toward her throat.

Neta was on her feet now, her face white, her eyes wild with terror. "Jim," she whispered, "Jim!" I could see her whole body trembling as she tried to break the ropes of terror that held her. "Jim," she said again.

But already the darkness was sliding into my head. I seemed to lose my balance and stumble forward again. My hands were already at her throat. Then with a last terrific struggle of consciousness I dived at Roger Swanson.

"Hold me," I yelled at him. "Keep me away from her." My arms were already around him when I saw the light gleam on his right hand and a new, unbearable terror smashed into me.

For his right hand was made of steel, the fingers long and hooked. In that instant I knew who had killed McDavid and Bill Jones!

The heavy steel hand swung up, slashed at my head. But I was close to him and the blow landed glancingly on the back of my neck. Then my left hand closed on the steel.

I had five inches more height and forty pounds more weight than Roger Swanson. I tore at his arm, snatched it from behind my neck and jabbed it at his own throat—forced it against his gullet, with all my superior strength. Instinctively, he tried to snatch his hand away. The steel fingers struck like a hawk's claw, buried

themselves in his throat. With the last blind reeling of my consciousness, I tried to tear the hand from his neck. I saw the flesh burst, the wild gush of blood.

I heard Neta's shrill, hysterical scream smashing against the cell, and I felt the rush of warm blood over my face. After that there was nothing but oblivion. . . .

BECAUSE of Roger Swanson's death, the whole thing was never explained as clearly as it might have been. The police, however, brought out all the necessary details. For a long time after the investigation, which resulted in the killings being pinned on Roger, and subsequently in my release from prison, even the police were baffled by Roger's motive. It was not until after they had sought out my uncle, Paul Farlan—the wealthy and eccentric recluse—for whom Roger acted as secretary, that his purpose became clear.

Kinship is close in my family; so Uncle Paul had willed Roger enough money for him to live on. But Roger, the police learned, already owed that much. My uncle had divided the rest of his estate into three equal portions, One part was to come to me. The rest was to go to the two men whom Uncle Paul had decided were winning the most promising literary careers of anyone in the state and who needed the money. Because he never read the newspapers it is not likely that he would ever have been aware of their deaths. The old man spent most of his time reading books, but he would not allow a newspaper or magazine into his home.

He did, however, hear of my conviction as a murderer, because Uncle Wade told him. It was then that he changed his will, leaving my share to Neta, who was the only person that he really cared for. And while he was making this

32

change, it occurred to him that the other two beneficiaries might die; and he inserted a clause leaving their share to charity under such conditions.

This meant that Roger would get nothing at all except his own share unless Neta were killed. And so Roger tried that last desperate attempt in the jail. When he first originated his plans, the will was so phrased that by eliminating the beneficiaries the entire estate would have been divided between Roger and my Uncle Wade who were the only living relatives. Uncle Wade was an old man and could not have lived much longer.

We never learned just what kind of knockout drops he was using on me. I am sure, however, that they were administered earlier, and that the odor immediately preceding each attack was some kind of catalytic agent which speeded up the reaction. The last dose he gave me must have been in the flask from which he only pretended to drink. I don't know when he administered the others, but a man drinks plenty in a roadhouse.

Concerning the dream, I have never been certain. I had probably been doped before going to sleep and then, during those half stupified moments when I was coming out from the effects of the drugs, a picture of the statue which I was to see

later may have been flashed against the dark wall of the room.

The steel glove which Roger used had fingers which worked on the same principle as ice tongs; the harder he pulled away, the deeper the fingers dug in. It was because of this that he was killed when I tried to pull the hand from his throat.

We were never able to locate the Chinese whom he had hired to help him, though the police are still working on the idea that it was the Chinese who modeled the wax statues with my face and the faces of the victims. They did find, however, the trap doors by which he caused the statues to appear and disappear, and the electric wires which he had rigged up so that from several places inside the dining room he could disconnect the entire light service.

The blue marks are still on the back of my hand. They must have been stamped there by tiny tattoo needles, probably set in a rubber stamp, during the brief moments when I was unconscious. I don't know. But I do know that now, whenever I look at them and then look up to see my wife's eyes watching me, I feel the swift surge of terror, the cold fear sweeping along my spine. And I shall never forget these things. I cannot look at those blue lines and at Neta's white throat without shuddering. . . .

THE END

COMING NEXT ISSUE!

Why did the killer, sating his blood-lust in the dark, prey only upon those nearest and dearest to Matthew Haley? Who would next keep a ghastly midnight rendezvous with the black-clad intruder— whose evil gift was sudden, agonizing death?

MR. MORGAN BELZAK, senior partner of the Belzak-Haley Department Stores, Inc., paced slowly down the first-floor corridor of the Peterboro Apartments, produced a ring of keys from a pocket of his oxford-gray overcoat and let himself into apartment number seven. Extending a plump hand to the light-switch near the door, he thumbed it awkwardly, then closed the door behind him and paraded into the expensively furnished living room.

A clock on the living room mantle said three A. M., and Morgan Belzak hiccoughed noisily as he peered at it. The lateness of the hour did not trouble him. Yesterday the auditors had checked the books of the Belzak-Haley Company, and the figures had revealed a profit for the first time in three years. Morgan Belzak had determined to celebrate the occasion. He had done so. Now he was quite drunk.

Devils in the Dark

by

HUGH B. CAVE

Author of "Dark Slaughter," etc.

Feature=Length Mystery Novel

With middle-aged sluggishness he removed his coat and hat and placed them on the somber-hued divan at one end of the room. His suit-coat and necktie he draped over the back of a chair before scuffing into the kitchen and pouring himself a drink. Glass in hand, he returned to the living room and sat at the antique mahogany desk in the corner.

He sat there a long while before remembering his reason for doing so. Then he finished his drink, made a face over the empty glass, and pawed open the center drawer of the desk. His companion for the best part of the evening had been a charming young lady who had begun by being a stranger and ended by being something far more entertaining. He had promised to send her a check.

Laboriously he unscrewed the cap of his fountain pen, opened the checkbook, and looked at the desk calendar in front of him to make sure of the date. He did not hear the almost inaudible tread of naked feet behind him. He did not turn to see the hunch-shouldered, black-cloaked figure which moved softly toward him from the doorway leading to the dining room.

Boring eyes studied the back of Morgan Belzak's stooped head. Gaunt hands rose slowly upward to the level of the unsuspecting man's neck. Had Belzak turned, had he looked into the contorted face of the cloaked menace behind him, he might have stumbled erect in time to escape. But he did not turn. He was concerned only with the checkbook in front of him, and with the failure of his fountain pen to operate properly.

The cloaked figure came to a stop directly behind him and stood there, glaring down hungrily. Hooked fingers hung above Belzak's neck, then shot forward with uncanny quickness and fastened in soft flesh. The doomed man had no chance. He stiffened, and a single short grunt escaped his throat; then he was dragged backward and hurled to the floor. And the cloaked figure fell upon him.

Morgan Belzak looked up into the face of his assailant, and screamed. His wide-open eyes saw white, tight-drawn skin, carmine lips and sunken cheeks. Frantically he tore at the murderous hands which encircled his throat. Madly he strove to free himself from the weight of his assailant's body. Then the hooked

fingers fastened deeper in his neck; the white face descended triumphantly with gaping mouth. Cruel teeth sank into him. His lurid scream became a gurgle, and ended in silence.

The clock on the mantel ticked on, its big hand moving sluggishly across five spaces, then five more—and five more.

Finally the cloaked figure stood erect, gazing down at Morgan Belzak's dead body. A soft, triumphant laugh echoed in the silent room. Slowly, unemotionally the intruder turned and paced to the door through which Belzak had entered the apartment twenty minutes before.

The door opened, closed silently. On the mantel, the clock ticked on relentlessly. Morgan Belzak lay alone in death, his throat ripped open, his eyes fixed wide with horror—his body drained of blood.

CHAPTER TWO

Beyond Return

A COLD, raw wind swept across the Brookline Reservoir and clawed angrily at Stephen Wayne's bent body as he paced uphill along the half-cleared sidewalk of Verne Street. New England, in January, could be vicious, despite the hypocritical ballyhoo of native New Englanders who kept one eye shut and wore a rose-colored glass over the other. Here in Chestnut Hill, amid expensive homes of upper-crust Bostonians January could be an excellent advertisement to lure normal young men to healthier climes. The fact that many of the expensive homes were closed and shuttered, abandoned for the winter, was proof of that!

Stephen Wayne, trudging along Verne Street with both hands wedged deep in the pockets of his raglan overcoat, hat-brim pulled down to shield his frowning features, thought grimly of southern resorts and wondered if the loveliness and

36

charm of twenty-two year old Gloria Haley were really of sufficient weight to balance the discomforts of Boston's unruly climate. He, Stephen Wayne, was in Boston because Gloria Haley had begged him to remain—and because the sight of the murdered, mutilated body of Morgan Belzak, erstwhile partner and business associate of Gloria Haley's church-loving, widowed father, had aroused the bloodhound instincts which had lain dormant in Steve Wayne ever since he had deserted police headquarters and become a private "investigator" who seldom allowed business to interfere with pleasure.

"I'm afraid!" Gloria had said, putting out a trembling hand to cling to Steve's arm. "I'm afraid, Steve! Why should anyone want to kill Belzak that way? If it was for business reasons, then my father may be in danger, too. You've got to help me, Steve!"

No man could have refused; least of all Steve Wayne, who, despite his mania for running around the country—or perhaps because of that mania—was amazingly susceptible to feminine allure. Moreover he knew the Haleys well, had known them for years, had even on several occasions asked Gloria Haley to say something more than: "Well, maybe someday, Steve." So now, at nine A. M., an unearthly hour for Steve Wayne to be up and abroad, he was parading down Verne Street toward the big brown house on the corner of Porter.

He scowled again when he looked up at the mansion-like structure. Strangely enough, the front path had not been cleared of snow, and was beaten solid by the imprint of many feet. The door hung open. Loose snow had drifted across the threshold into the hallway.

He climbed the steps slowly, put a finger on the bell, and walked in. Voices were audible from the far end of the cor-

ridor. He strode forward, wondering why Mannix, the butler, had not made a hurried appearance at the bell's shrill clamor.

Mannix did make an appearance then. He was a short fat man, attired in gloomy black which accentuated the smoothness of his pate, and he came jerkily from the library, blinking his eyes and rubbing his hands together as if to warm them.

He said: "Oh, it's you Mr. Wayne!" and seemed more at ease. Something had happened to disturb his usually undisturbable attitude of slow-footed efficiency. He even looked afraid.

Steve peered at him critically and said, "Where's Miss Haley?"

"She's in the librar—" The butler checked himself. "If you'll wait in the back study, sir, I'll tell her you're here."

Steve nodded, shot a sharp glance at the man and walked down the dark, drafty corridor. He knew the Haley house well. Built in the late 'eighties by Haley's father, the present owner had left it untouched, excepting for the substitution of electricity for gas-light. Rambling, and dismal, it was furnished with the elaborate gimcrackery of a bygone age. Empty, armored figures loomed from the dark corners of the hall; massive furniture, like huge, sleeping animals crouched in the gloomy interior.

Steve Wayne noticed that the folding double doors of the library were closed; and as he passed, curious, he caught the glint of the metal lock in the crack between the doors. From within came the sound of hushed voices. Although the words w e r e indistinguishable, Steve Wayne stopped, ears alert, nerves tingling.

There was no mistaking it—stark fear and horror came to him in the tense tones of those lowered voices.

JAW set, Steve stepped forward. He knew that the library opened into the next room beyond, and he was just turn-

37

ing into it when a heavy hand grasped his shoulder. He whirled to see Mannix' fat, sweat-beaded face close to his own. "My God, Mister Wayne, don't—" And the man seemed to recover himself. "Pardon me, sir. Mr. Haley's strict orders are that no one is to go inside the library." His voice was desperate, pleading. "Please, sir, the back study—"

Gray, steel-like eyes bored into the butler's fear-filled pupils. "Okay, Mannix. But what the hell—?"

The distant echo of a bell-pull sounded. Mannix wet his lips. "Yes, sir. The back study—" and was off to answer the summons.

Steve swore under his breath, hesitated, and then with a shrug of his broad shoulders entered the gloomy room to which he had been directed.

A dim yellow bulb seemed to accentuate the gloom more than to dispel it. The place was packed with a weird assortment of furniture. A priceless Adam highboy was jammed against a huge ruffled davenport; mission oak mingled with Sheraton pieces, and velvet drapes with fringed lambrequins seemed to hang from every conceivable corner. Shadows, and a musty, airless smell....

Steve shook himself, as if to ward off an evil spell wrought by the gloom. Although it was warm enough there, he felt an uncomfortable chill race down his spine.

He got up from his chair and moved toward the curtained aperture which should, he knew, open onto the room adjoining the library. And then, his hand on the door-knob, he paused. Footsteps sounded beyond the closed door. Two pairs of feet, advancing slowly into that adjoining room.

From beyond the closed door Matthew Haley's gruff voice raised suddenly in anger.

"You can't have her, Ebbarton—you

hear me? You can't have her now. You —you're too late."

There came the creak of a chair, and another voice spoke evenly.

"Did it ever occur to you, Matthew, that I might be able to give the police some interesting information about your ancestors—information which might have direct bearing on the death of Morgan Belzak?"

Steve Wayne, listening beyond the door, stiffened. He could imagine Matthew Haley's gaunt eyes flashing fire.

There was a moment of silence—silence that hung freighted with tension. Then, in a perfectly expressionless tone, Haley said, "You've let self-sympathy unbalance your mind, Ebbarton. You— you abused Julia when she was your wife. Do you think any such foolish charge against me would bring her back to you now?"

The chair creaked again, and the man addressed as Ebbarton spoke pleadingly. "I'm giving you this chance, Haley, merely because, like a damned fool, I'm sentimental. We were friends once— good ones! Until you literally stole my wife. She—got a divorce, of course. And now you're—going to marry her!" His voice was bitter, somehow pitiable.

Suddenly then he cried out harshly, "Well—I want her back! You understand? The past two years I've lost everything—my wife—all my money. Damn the money. But Julia—damn it, Haley, I need her! I'm not young any more—"

His voice was thick, emotion-choked.

Matthew Haley laughed, and his words were measured, mingling loathing and contempt: "You—miserable—blackmailer!" he said.

Ebbarton's voice, when he answered, was increasingly hysterical. "She loves me, damn you! *Me*—understand! You—

38

you've done something to her—changed her in some frightful way—"

"She came to me of her own accord, as you well know," Haley said calmly. "Came because she couldn't stand your torturing her. My God! You should know. I saw the unhealed scars on her arms, on her neck—"

"I have a beastly temper. She's high-strung as hell—so'm I. But I swear to you! Oh, for God's sake, send her back to me, Matthew!"

Matthew Haley said nothing.

"All right. All right! I gave you your chance." Steve Wayne heard Ebbarton getting up from his chair, moving across the floor toward the hall door. "My attorneys will notify you the first thing Monday morning, Matthew. I'm starting suit against you for alienation."

"Alienation of affections? On account of—Julia?" Matthew Haley's voice was dangerously soft.

"Yes. For one hundred thousand dollars. And—and, by God! when I get it, I'll take the check and turn it over to any charity you name—badly as I need the money. 'Blackmail,' you said! Ahh!"

Haley's voice, when he spoke again, seemed that of an old, broken man.

"John," he said, "that—that suit would be quite useless. I no longer have Julia's affections. She—she's left me!"

Ebbarton grunted. "Left you?" he echoed. "Good God! Where—when—"

Matthew Haley spoke slowly. "Julia," he said, "was murdered sometime last night. It is ghastly—horrible— Her throat—" He stopped, controlled himself. "She met her death, John, in the identical manner that Morgan Belzak met his. Come into the library."

SWEAT stood out on Steve Wayne's brow as the footfalls of the two men diminished. He stood up slowly, grasping the back of a chair. Julia Ebbarton the

second victim! Who would be next? What was this horrible fate that wreaked its terrifying, bloody murder upon those who stood close to Matthew Haley?

Quick, light footfalls sounded outside the hall door. Swiftly Steve crossed to it, unlocked it. Gloria, strikingly beautiful in crimson and black lounging pajamas stood there. He could see that she was suffering under a strain; lack of sleep had made her eyes unusually bright; lines of nervousness were about her mouth. But her chin was up.

She smiled. "Mannix said you were waiting. Sorry, Steve, I couldn't get away— Then she stopped, reading something intuitively in Steve's face. "You—you've heard it?" she shuddered. "Ugh—it's like a nightmare! And—damn it—I'm afraid, Steve. Afraid for father!"

He put a reassuring hand upon her arm. His voice was clipped. "You—and he are all right, Gloria. I'm going into the library. Don't come unless you want to."

But she walked with him, her eyes wide, her face pale. "Thank God you've come, Steve!" she whispered.

The inner library door was open. Steve stood on the threshold, staring. Inside the richly furnished room half a dozen people were assembled. Matthew Haley and another man his own age—evidently Ebbarton—were there, bent over something that lay on the divan. Two uniformed policemen stood awkwardly by a heavy, walnut table. A servant girl was gaping at Inspector Frank Moody of Headquarters, who was parading importantly up and down the luxurious Persian rug. For a moment no one was aware of Steve's presence.

He paced forward and stared at the thing on the divan. His own eyes widened, and he stood rigid a moment before advancing to Matthew Haley's side. Then he gazed down in horror at the woman's half-naked body, shuddering involuntarily.

The rather attractive divorced wife of John Ebbarton lay there, her sightless eyes staring at the ceiling. Her plump body was torn, hideously mangled. Her face was a mask of utter terror; her eyes dilated, her mouth frozen open. Her throat was ripped horribly, just as the throat of Morgan Belzak had been ripped.

Slowly John Ebbarton rose to his feet, walked to the door of the room. Then the front door closed with a muffled thud.

STEVE made fists of his hands, shoved them solidly against his hips, and stood staring. His mind played with the problem, sorting out those elements which seemed important, and holding them up for mental examination. Here was a mystery horrible enough to make even Steve Wayne shudder, and Steve, despite the fact that his years of life numbered only twenty-six, was not unfamiliar with murder in its most gruesome forms. His hankering for things unusual and dangerous had taken him into more than one strange maze.

He looked at Inspector Moody, and Moody said nothing. Moody was no half-wit, either. He had a brain, knew how to use it. But this business evidently had him stumped. As for the others, the two cops were still minding their own business, Matthew Haley was standing motionless by the divan, the servant girl was still gaping goggle-eyed, and Gloria was looking expectantly at Steve.

"When did it happen?" Steve demanded.

Haley made a choking sound in his throat and mumbled thickly: "Last night —sometime. I—I found her this morning when I went to call her for breakfast. She was my guest, and—"

And she was the woman Haley loved. That was important. Morgan Belzak had been Haley's partner, and this woman would soon have been Haley's wife. Someone, some inhuman fiend who fed on horror, had deliberately wiped out the two persons who occupied first and second place in Haley's esteem. First and second? Well, maybe. There was Gloria. Steve glanced at her and felt suddenly afraid for her. She was Haley's daughter. Unless he was guessing wrong, she was in horrible danger.

He strode to her side and drew her toward the door. She let him lead her into the corridor; then she leaned against the wall and stared at him helplessly.

"What can we do, Steve?"

"Tell me what you know."

"I—I don't know anything. Mrs. Ebbarton was staying here for the weekend. This morning father went to her room to call her for breakfast, and—and I heard him scream. I ran upstairs and found him kneeling beside her. She was dead, Steve. Then I called the police. Father didn't want me to, but I did it anyway. And Inspector Moody came, with the policemen, and they carried the body downstairs, and—that's all."

Steve nodded, and looked up sharply as the servant girl appeared in the doorway. The girl was a blonde, with saucer eyes and a scared, thin face. She came forward timidly. She had worked for the Haley's more than a year now. Her name was Olga something, and she was supposed to be Hungarian. Haley had a yen for foreigners.

The girl licked her lips and said: "Please, sir, can I speak with you alone? It's about—about the thing that killed Mrs. Ebbarton."

Steve glanced at Gloria. Gloria frowned and said: "She has some foolish idea. She tried to tell it to Inspector Moody, and he wouldn't listen."

The servant girl put a hand on Steve's

arm. Steve shrugged, drew her aside, waited for her to speak. She licked her lips again and began to talk jerkily, hoarsely:

"Yes, sir, I did try to tell Inspector Moody, and I know what I'm talking about! It isn't long since I came to this country, and I haven't forgot all I knew before I come here. Maybe you don't believe in vampires, but I do. I've lived where they are, and people are feared of them. And it was a vampire that killed Mrs. Ebbarton! No one else would have drunk all the blood out of her body like that!"

The girl's eyes were full of genuine terror. Steve looked into them and saw something else—saw the mental images behind the terror. Maybe she was right; maybe Belzak and the Ebbarton woman had been murdered by the kind of monster she had in mind. Not the legendary type of vampire, not the blood-eating, dead-alive vampire who crawled from its grave at sunset and feasted on death during the hours of darkness, but a human fiend with vampirical tendencies. Stranger things were written in the big red book, and they were not superstitious claptrap either, but cold fact.

Steve said: "All right, sister. Thanks."

He strode back into the library and found Gloria waiting for him. She took his hand, looked into his face.

"You'll stay here, Steve? You won't leave me?"

"You're right I'll stay," he scowled.

He meant it, even though Matthew Haley was staring at him queerly and coming forward to talk to him. Matthew Haley, religious and methodical in his mode of living had always frowned upon Steve's life-is-what-you-make-it-and-to-hell-with-the-consequences attitude. Haley and Steve Wayne were not the best of friends.

CHAPTER THREE

The Clock Ticks On

AFTER the simple funeral ceremony, held in the Haley house the following day, Steve and Gloria accompanied Matthew Haley to the cemetery. A cheerless cold sleet was blowing up from Boston Harbor as they drove through the ornate iron gateway.

Red-eyed from lack of sleep, following his night's vigil in the house, Steve stood with the little group as the minister read the last words over the remains of Julia Ebbarton. For a moment they bowed their heads and Steve, glancing toward Matthew Haley, noted how he had aged in that one night. And suddenly, he was aware of a strange sound behind him—a muffled sob—and yet not quite that.

He turned, to see the peculiarly thin face of John Ebbarton, now twisted in grief. Ebbarton seemed to move as a man in a dream. He came close to Matthew Haley, standing at one side of Steve. Even though Steve moved away, guiding Gloria back toward the car, he heard the disconnected words from Ebbarton's lips.

"Sorry—must have been crazy yesterday, Matthew.... It's hell, I guess.... both of us . . . . Will you—?"

And Steve turned in time to see John Ebbarton's outstretched hand clasped by Matthew Haley. And then, in a moment Ebbarton was gone, striding swiftly toward a waiting taxi.

Steve and Gloria watched it pull away with him, and Steve noted the steamer trunk lashed on the rear, and the heavy suitcases piled beside the driver.

"Strange!" he muttered. And at Gloria's question, he told her of what he had overheard in the back study the day before.

She shuddered. "It—it's so horrible, Steve! We used to know John Ebbarton so very well. Until—father always

41

thought he was abusing Julia. That he—was tired of her. Julia has always been so swell, but so damned unlucky. Even to the—last. I was always awfully fond of both of them, but I liked Julia better...."

She shuddered, clung closer to Steve, as they waited for Matthew Haley. "It's too bad, I think, that John Ebbarton couldn't have gone away—before Julia died. I can't help but think he tried to hound her—make her return to him. She wasn't looking well before—before it happened."

Steve grinned. "Silly! You're just nervous—over-tired. Forget the whole thing, if you can, Gloria. I'll fix you a hot drink when we get home...."

But Steve Wayne, as he tried to comfort the girl, hoped that his voice carried more confidence than he felt.

THE clock in the Haley library ticked on relentlessly, just as the clock in Morgan Belzak's apartment had ticked while measuring the moments of Belzak's life. The hour was nine-thirty. Steve Wayne paced slowly down the corridor, stepped over the library threshold, and stood staring.

The room contained only one occupant. Matthew Haley sat there in a straight-backed chair before the huge brick fireplace—sat with his head bowed in his hands, his eyes closed, his graying hair gleaming dully in the light of the bridge-lamp behind him. His lips were mumbling words, and the words, in this house of death, seemed strangely out of place, strangely macabre.

"Our Father who art in Heaven .... hallowed be Thy name ...."

Steve stood motionless, listening, scowling. Mechanically he pulled the glowing cigarette from his lips and held it in a dangling hand. The smoke from the white cylinder curled upward slowly, flattening out as it reached the ceiling; and Matthew Haley's droning voice continued to send up its prayer.

".... and forgive us our trespasses, as we forgive those who ...."

The voice died to a whisper and became silent. Haley lifted his head, made a soft sighing sound. Then he saw Steve and stiffened guiltily, as if ashamed of himself. Steve paced forward, pulled up a chair, and sat down.

"You've thought over what I told you, Mr. Haley?"

Haley stared, moved his head up and down slowly. "I've thought about it, but —but I can't think of a single person."

"Think again. Someone, somewhere, has a grudge against you. That's the only lead we can work on."

"But I tell you, I don't know any such man."

Steve thought of John Ebbarton, and scowled. He wet the end of his cigarette and sucked on it with tight lips. Everything depended on Haley; yet the man had spent the whole day pacing helplessly about the house, refusing to speak unless spoken to. He was afraid; that was obvious. His face had grown pale; his eyes were red and watery; even now he was trembling and gripping the chair-arms with gaunt, bloodless hands.

"What did Moody say? Anything?"

"No, nothing," Haley mumbled. "He —he said he didn't know what to think. He and his men took Mrs. Ebbarton away, and he promised to come back tomorrow."

"And you can't think of a single person who might want to do you harm?"

"No—I can't."

Steve scowled again and studied the man intently. Maybe Haley was lying, but the possibility seemed remote. The fear in those eyes was too genuine; the haggard, strained expression of that tired face was no mere mask.

42

"You'd better go to bed," Steve said quietly.

Haley stood up as if welcoming the suggestion.

"Is—is my daughter in bed?"

"Half an hour ago."

"Very well then," Haley mumbled. "I —I can do nothing by staying up. I— good-night, Wayne."

STEVE sat alone, listening to the monotonous tick of the clock. He heard Haley walk slowly down the corridor and climb the stairs to the floor above. The silence of the house magnified every footstep, every creak of the floor. A door opened, closed dully. Then the silence was complete.

Steve stood up, turned out the light, and sat down again. He had no intention of going to bed; not yet anyway. Whoever had murdered Belzak and Mrs. Ebbarton would undoubtedly aim the next blow at someone else closely associated with Haley. Perhaps it would not happen tonight or even tomorrow night, but it would certainly happen eventually. There was nothing to be gained by going to bed, going to sleep, and waking in the morning to find a third horrible victim with its throat ripped open and the blood drained from its veins.

The clock ticked on endlessly, counting seconds into minutes, minutes into eternities. Steve took a cigarette and box of matches from his pocket, then scowled, thrust the matches back, and chewed on the cigarette without lighting it. No sound at all invaded Haley's big house. The place was a monstrous tomb, still and dark. The servants, four of them in all, had retired long ago to their quarters in the left wing. Upstairs, Gloria Haley and her father were asleep in their rooms—or at least trying to sleep.

More than an hour had passed since Haley had gone upstairs.

Steve stood up, frowning. The business of waiting was enough to tighten any man's nerves, especially the nerves of a man who preferred action to aimless suspense. He put a hand in his pocket, brought out a small circular flashlight. Holding the light down and cupping it with his palm, so that its glow played over the carpet in front of him, he paced silently into the corridor. It would do no harm, and might do some good, to have a look at Haley's house while its occupants were asleep. Houses sometimes possessed souls of their own.

He moved noiselessly down the corridor, past the wide staircase. Glancing up at the well of gloom above, he thought of Gloria Haley lying asleep in her bed, and felt suddenly grateful that he had obeyed the impulse to remain in Boston. The girl needed protection. She could not get it from her father; that was sure. Matthew Haley preferred to put his trust in the Lord. That was all right, too—but Steve Wayne believed a loaded revolver, a pair of tough fists, and a fast-working brain were necessary in this case.

He prowled past the staircase, and his flashlight shone dully on a closed door at the end of the passage. The door led to the kitchen. He moved toward it. Then he stood stock still, his feet glued to the carpet and his lips clamped shut on the unlighted cigarette which protruded between them.

At the top of the staircase a floor-board had creaked ominously. Slow footsteps were audible in the upstairs corridor!

For ten seconds Steve stood rigid, listening. Then his eyes narrowed triumphantly, his lips curled. The suspense was done with now; it was a time for action, swift and decisive. The fiend responsible for Belzak's death, and the death of Matthew Haley's intended wife, had blundered, had been fool enough to return before the hue and cry had subsided!

Noiselessly Steve gained the foot of the staircase and began to ascend. His groping hand slid upward along the smooth bannister; his other hand slipped into his pocket, released the flashlight, and closed over a small automatic. If it came to a showdown, Steve Wayne knew how to use that automatic—had used it before, with deadly results, in emergencies such as this!

Halfway up the stairs he stopped, stood listening again. No sound was audible above, but after a ten-second interval of ugly silence, a significant noise came from the far end of the upstairs hall. It was hard to tabulate, that noise. It sounded like the muffled thud of bare feet parading over a wooden floor.

Steve climbed warily, revolver ready in case he needed it. He thought grimly of the horrible deaths which had overtaken the killer's two victims, and the thought caused his fingers to tighten viciously around the gun-butt. Then he reached the head of the staircase and stood motionless, trying vainly to see through the pall of darkness which enshrouded the upper corridor.

THE sound of naked feet had ceased. The corridor was still as a vault. Slowly, deliberately Steve moved down it, staring straight ahead of him and hugging the wall.

He traversed half the length of the black passage before he stopped again; then he stiffened, jerked his revolver up, and stood trembling. Something, some unseen, unnamable shape, had moved in the darkness ahead of him, creating a soft whisper which was almost no sound at all. That whisper was the almost inaudible sigh of breath emanating from human lips.

Steve's eyes narrowed, grew hard. Slowly he snaked a hand into his pocket and brought out the tiny flashlight. He set himself. The light snapped on, stabbing a pale ocher shaft through the dark.

Steve stood stiff, then, and sucked air through his curled lips. The flashlight's eye revealed a crouching, bare-footed figure not more than ten paces distant. Even as the light struck it, the figure straightened and whirled, glaring savagely into Steve's face. Steve saw the man's contorted features, recognized them. The man's hand was still half extended toward the door of Matthew Haley's room.

There was no hesitation. A growl of triumph welled from Steve's throat as he hurtled forward. He made no attempt to use the revolver in his hand; he wanted the killer alive. The man made a desperate effort to escape. Violently he leaped backward, pawing the wall to steady himself. Then he was down, locked in the crushing embrace of Steve's arms—down and writhing, fighting furiously to free himself.

He was no weakling. He knew tricks, used them. Sharp teeth sank into Steve's shoulder, imbedding themselves in agonized flesh. A stiff forefinger jabbed up with lightning speed and would have found a mark in Steve's throat if Steve had not lunged sideways the moment before contact. Sullenly, silently the killer strove to free himself and escape, while his hot breath assailed Steve's nostrils and his wiry body turned and twisted with snake-like rapidity.

Then he made a mistake. In the midst of his efforts he lay suddenly still, feigning defeat only to bring his knee up with crushing force and bury it in Steve's groin. Steve grunted, bent double with pain. The killer leaped erect, hesitated, swung his naked foot back to kick viciously at Steve's face.

Steve's hands shot out and clamped

around the bare ankle. A single upward thrust threw the man off balance. He stumbled, went down in a grotesque heap. Steve's clenched fist ground into that snarling mouth even before the twisted head slapped the floor. A long sigh welled from the killer's lips, and he lay still, moaning.

Steve struggled erect, then, and stood swaying, breathing in gasps. A full minute passed before he stooped and groped for the fallen flashlight; then he clicked the light on and looked both ways along the corridor. The door of Matthew Haley's room was still closed; so was the door of the adjoining room, in which Gloria lay asleep. Steve scowled, walked to the first door and stood listening. No sound came from within. Evidently the noise of conflict had not penetrated that heavy barrier, or else Haley's weariness and run-down condition had caused the man to sleep abnormally well.

But not so with Haley's daughter. The adjoining door opened while Steve was pacing back to the slumped shape on the floor. He turned abruptly, flashlight held rigid. In the doorway the girl stood facing him, staring at him fearfully.

She came forward slowly, indecision and fright stamped on her face. No doubt she had heard every separate sound of the disturbance, and had waited helplessly for the sounds to identify themselves. She was trembling now, as Steve's hand found her arm to steady her. Her white silk pajamas made her look like something unreal, fantastic. She turned a pale, strained face toward the thing on the floor and said almost inaudibly:

"What—what is it, Steve?"

Steve hesitated, then said deliberately: "Nothing. Nothing for you to worry about."

"But—"

"I'll take care of it, downstairs. Go back to bed."

Gloria took a step forward and looked down into the upturned face of the man who had attempted to invade her father's room. Steve pulled his flashlight away too slowly. She saw the face, recognized it, stiffened fearfully. It was a bloody face now, its mouth crushed and swollen, its eyes dilated. Not pretty to look at.

"Mannix—" she said slowly. "Steve, it's Mannix—"

STEVE nodded grimly. The man on the floor was Mannix, the butler, the man who had served Matthew Haley for years. He had been the last man open to suspicion, had seemed utterly harmless. It was unbelievable, but—

"Go back to bed," Steve ordered again, more firmly. "You can't do anything. None of us can, until Moody gets here in the morning. I'll take care of this."

He pushed past her and bent down, lifting the butler's limp body in his arms. Deliberately he walked down the corridor, leaving the girl to stand and stare at him. At the head of the stairs he turned, looked back, then scowled and descended to the lower floor. Mannix was a dead weight, unconscious.

Steve carried him into the library, dumped him into a chair, and turned on a light. There was nothing particularly vicious about the man's appearance. His plump body was soft and limp, his face battered and bruised. But it was better to take precautions and make the man secure. Only a short while ago he had been fighting like a madman; he might do so again at the first opportunity.

Steve strode into the hall then, and turned on more lights. Still scowling, he paced into the kitchen and look around him, seeking something with which to bind the butler's arms and legs. There was no proof, yet, that Mannix had murdered Morgan Belzak and Mrs. Ebbarton; but circumstantial evidence was sufficient to turn the man over to the police.

A thick coil of rope, evidently a clothesline, hung from a nail in the corner. Steve took it, carried it back to the library. With no attempt to be gentle, he jerked the butler's legs together and bound them, passing the rope several times around the chair-legs. Then he secured the man's arms, stood back, and stared grimly into the still unconscious face.

And then he forgot Mannix, forgot the affair of the upstairs corridor, and stood utterly rigid. In his ears jangled a sound which struck fear to his heart and caused his eyes to widen with abnormal quickness.

The sound came from the rear of the house, from the direction of the servants' quarters. Like a living entity it shrilled through the corridor, eating its way into the room where Steve stood.

It was a lurid scream of absolute terror, and it came from a woman's lips!

CHAPTER FOUR

Devil in the Dark

FOR ten seconds that scream of terror left Steve helpless. He stared mutely at Mannix, stared at the door leading to the corridor. Dully he realized that he had guessed wrong, made a terrible mistake. Next moment he was in the hall, running recklessly toward the kitchen.

The scream was not repeated, and the grim silence of the house drove caution into Steve's tormented mind before he had traversed the corridor's length. Reaching the kitchen, where he had left a light burning less than five minutes ago, he advanced warily, tensely. His hand was no longer trembling when it reached out to open the door leading to the servants' quarters. His eyes were narrowed, unblinking, his lips drawn tight in a downward scowl.

The narrow passage extending before him was lightless and he paced down it without touching the light-switch in the wall. Then he stopped, aware that the silence was no longer complete. A vague, unnamable sound emanated from the darkness ahead of him. He moved forward slowly, noiselessly; and the sound increased in volume as he neared its source.

No faintest ray of light relieved the blackness of the passage. The place was dead, lifeless, except for that significant sound. And the sound itself was hideous, ugly, suggestive of things better left alone. Somewhere ahead, in the dark, an animal was feeding hungrily—or was it an animal? Steve did not know. Grimly he advanced, striving to see what lay before him.

He came upon the thing before he expected to. Came upon it abruptly, and would have stumbled headlong into the room where the horror was being enacted, had he not caught himself in time. Prowling along the passage, feeling his way with an outstretched hand, he encountered an open doorway. His groping hand, deprived of the support of the wall, lunged into empty space and threw him off balance. He steadied himself by gripping the sides of the door-frame. Then his gaze focused on the room's contents, and he dragged a quick, rasping breath through his teeth.

The room was a small one, dimly lighted by pale moon-glow emanating from a narrow window. An iron bed angled out from the corner, its white-enameled posts and white sheets gleaming dully in the pale illumination. Beside the bed and half crouched, a black-robed shape loomed out in strange contrast. And the black-robed thing was feeding.

The thing did not turn. Evidently it had not heard the muffled sounds accompanying Steve's impromptu entrance.

46

It was concerned only with the limp lifeless shape beneath it. That shape was a woman's body.

Steve stared, horrified. Dully he realized that he was too late; the horror had already been enacted; the woman on the bed, half naked, her nightgown ripped half off and her body exposed to the fiend's attack, was dead—mercifully so. And the black-robed monster who bent above her his vile lips sucking the hot blood from her mangled throat, was the monster who had murdered Morgan Belzak and Mrs. Ebbarton. No other answer was possible.

Steve's hand plunged jerkily into his pocket, seeking the revolver which lay there. He had witnessed horrible things before, but this was unbelievable, fantastic. He took a step forward, dragged the gun out. His whole body was shaking; his hand, holding the weapon, refused to be still. Savagely, gutturally, he rasped out the first words that came to his lips.

"Damn you, stop it! *Stop it!*"

The words had the effect of a whiplash. Like a montrous bat the blackrobed shape lunged clear of the bed, whirling on bent legs. For a split second the thing stood rigid. Its face was masked in shadow; its eyes smouldered like twin flames. Then a vicious hissing sound burst from its curled lips. With uncanny quickness the killer hurled himself forward.

Steve's gun belched once, then was rammed sideways. The bullet hit its mark, yet the murderer did not falter. White hands clawed at Steve's throat, hurling him backward. Gasping with amazement, he reeled into the wall, both fists beating a wild tattoo on the fiend's face. An odor of fresh blood assailed his nostrils, eating its way into his throat, choking him. He was fighting for his life and knew it—fighting with a monster who was human in form only. Any ordinary killer would have respected the deadly menace of a loaded revolver, would have cringed from it in fear. This black-robed being had not even hesitated, had flung himself forward so quickly, so furiously, that Steve had been caught off guard, stunned with amazement.

Now those gaunt hands were clawing Steve's face, drawing blood from torn flesh. That vile throat uttered deep, guttural growls like the rumblings of an enraged animal. Steve's clenched fists drove savagely, desperately into the fiend's chest and stomach, without effect.

Even as he fought, Steve realized that death was but a matter of moments. The room magnified every sound, hurling a torrent of noise into the corridor, just as it had hurled that first scream of terror from the lips of the woman who now lay dead on the bed. Locked in the monster's embrace, Steve stumbled backward, crashing violently against the bed-end, upsetting a small table which stood there with an unlighted lamp on it. His flailing legs caught in the rungs of a chair, upending it with a crash. He went down in a twisted heap, still fighting desperately, hopelessly, as the black-robed one fell upon him.

Then another sound filled the room, and over the monster's shoulder Steve saw a rigid shape standing in the doorway. The shape was a woman's—one of Matthew Haley's servant-girls. Her eyes were wide with horror, her hands uplifted as if to ward off the sight of the mangled victim on the bed and the robed horror in whose embrace Steve struggled. Wild shrieks rose from the woman's gaping mouth, drowning the guttural sounds of triumph which came from the monster's throat.

The grip on Steve's throat relaxed. Abruptly the black-robed fiend turned, stiffened. The next moment he was standing erect, snarling. Evidently the mind in that inhuman body was a cunning one, cunning enough to know that the tumult in the murder room had aroused the rest of the house. Ignoring Steve, the monster leaped toward the woman in the doorway. A vicious hand hurled the woman sideways. The doorway was suddenly full of a monsterous black shape; then it was empty again. The killer was gone.

THE woman was still screaming when Steve groped erect and stood swaying on braced legs. That hoarse screaming was music in Steve's ears. It had saved his life, saved him from the hideous death which had overtaken the pitiful thing on the bed. Sick at heart, nauseated by the stench of blood which clung to him, he stumbled into the corridor. His groping fingers found a light-switch; he walked unsteadily down the passage, realizing that his actions were merely mechanical and would avail nothing.

The monster had entered Matthew Haley's house without being intercepted. Doubtlessly he had left the same way. Without hope of success, Steve paced to the end of the corridor. An open door lay before him. He stood on the threshold and stared out into darkness, his fists clenched, his lips tight. The darkness was empty. The black-robed fiend was gone.

Slowly Steve walked back to the murder room. A light was burning, and the servant-woman was standing near the death-bed, staring mutely. Steve moved to the bed and looked down, then looked away again. He knew that the woman expected him to say something, but there was nothing to say. The near-naked body on the bed was the body of the Hungarian girl who had said, not long ago: "Maybe you don't believe in vampires, but I do. I've lived where they are. . . ."

Lived where they are! The words tortured Steve's memory. This pitiful thing on the bed, this girl named Olga something, had believed in a superstition. Now her own lifeless body, horribly mutilated and half drained of blood, presented grim proof that her beliefs had not been entirely wrong. The vampire-monster had struck thrice. Who would be his next victim?

Steve turned away and walked slowly to the door, motioning the servant-woman to follow him. The woman said feebly:

"What—what was it, sir? Oh God, what was it? I was asleep and I woke up thinkin' I heard a scream. Then I lay there, listenin', and after a long time I heard noises in Olga's room, and I got up to see what was wrong, and—"

Steve stood still, confronting her. The words "Go back to bed" came to his lips, and he stifled them. It was not safe, now, to send anyone back to bed.

"How many more servants sleep in the house?" he demanded grimly.

"None, sir. Mrs. Pelky, the housekeeper, she said she wouldn't sleep here tonight under any conditions, after what happened to Mrs. Ebbarton. She's staying in John's room up over the garage. John's the chauffeur, and it's his night off, so he's gone home to his folks."

"You and Olga were the only ones in the servants' quarters?"

"Yes, sir. Me and—and Olga. Oh my God, sir—I can't stay here now! After lookin' at what happened to her—"

"You'd better come with me," Steve said firmly.

Deliberately he strode down the corridor to the kitchen, with the woman trailing close behind him. The light in the kitchen was still burning; the room was empty. Closing the connecting door, he entered the main corridor leading to the front rooms. At the foot of the central staircase he stopped, looked up, frowned.

"Wait here," he said stiffly. "I'll be down in a moment with Miss Haley and her father. There'll be no more sleeping tonight."

Quickly he ascended the stairs and turned on a light in the upper hall, noting with relief that the doors of the bedrooms at the far end were closed. Stopping before the door of Gloria Haley's room, he knocked softly and waited impatiently for a response. Probably the girl was asleep. Certainly no sounds from the servants' quarters had penerated to this portion of the house to disturb her.

He knocked again and said quietly: "It's Steve. Open the door, Gloria." There was a sound of a bed creaking, then soft footsteps. The door opened slowly and he looked into the tense, frightened face of Matthew Haley's daughter.

"What is, it Steve? What's happened?"

He hesitated, said evenly: "Nothing. That is, nothing much. But I want you and your father to come downstairs."

She stared at him, evidently aware that he was lying for her benefit. He put a firm hand on her arm, returned her gaze without flinching, then said softly: "Better put a dressing gown or something over those pajamas," and turned away.

The door of Matthew Haley's room was but a few paces distant. He strode toward it, knocked. After a moment he scowled, knocked and knocked again. No answering sound came from within.

He knocked a fourth time, then put a hand on the knob and turned it. The door opened when he pushed. He stood on the threshold, stared into the lightless interior and said curtly:

"Haley!"

Then he realized that something was wrong. Quickly he felt for the light-switch, found it, and stood blinking in the sudden glare. His gaze encountered an empty bed with sheets thrown back in disarray. The room was empty. Matthew Haley was gone!

CHAPTER FIVE

One More Corpse

STEVE'S face lost color. Slowly he paced into Haley's room and stared around him, seeking some explanation of the man's disappearance. The bed had been slept in; that was certain. Yet the room contained no signs of violence. To all appearances Haley had retired for the night, then gotten up again and gone out. But where? Why?

Steve walked around the room, examined the bed, opened the closet door and peered past the line-up of suits hanging there. He strode to the single window and put a hand on the latch, satisfying himself that the window was locked—on the inside. Haley had not departed that way. Couldn't, anyway, unless he possessed uncanny athletic ability. The window overlooked a sheer drop of twenty feet to the ground!

Baffled, Steve moved out of the room. Gloria Haley was walking silently toward him, a heavy blue kimono wrapped tightly around her slim form. She saw the scowling expression of his face and spoke anxiously.

"Steve—"

He interrupted her curtly. "Your father's taken himself for a walk. Come downstairs."

Bewildered, she allowed herself to be led along the corridor and down the wide staircase to where the servant-woman was standing uneasily in the lower hall near the library door. Steve glanced at the door and remembered suddenly that he had left Mannix, the butler, bound to a chair in the room beyond. Striding to the threshold, he saw that the butler had not moved, had in fact, apparently resigned himself to his fate, and was sitting wearily with his eyes shut. He did not look up when the two women entered the room.

Steve faced the women grimly. They were a responsibility now, a handicap. He could not leave them alone in the house, after what had happened to the Hungarian girl. There was no telling when that black-robed fiend of darkness would return. No telling what abnormal powers the monster possessed.

Yet Matthew Haley had to be found. Fear had undoubtly caused Haley to abandon his room and seek the questionable safety of the outside. Safety? Even now the man might be wandering about the grounds or tramping the nearby streets, where his peril was infinitely greater!

A telephone lay on the library table. Steve strode to it, picked it up, worked the dial savagely with a rigid forefinger. He waited a long while for an answer, and glanced at Mannix while he waited. The butler was awake, staring at him sullenly, resentfully.

A voice came over the wire, and Steve said curtly: "Mollison there?"

The voice belonged to the deskman. Mollison—Captain Mollison of Headquarters, LaRonge Street—came to the phone a moment later and said quietly: "Yes?"

"Wayne speaking," Steve grunted. "Steve Wayne, at the Haley place. In need of help, Bob. There's been another murder."

Mollison made a rumbling sound in his throat, and Steve drew a mental picture of the man's face. It would be hard, inflexible under a mop of iron-gray hair, and Mollison would be scowling, pushing lean fingers through that gray mop. The newspapers had made a punching-bag of Mollison's department lately.

The words, "All right. I'll send a car over!" rasped into Steve's ear.

He lowered the phone and turned again to comfort Gloria Haley and the servant-woman. Gloria was sitting rigid, staring. She had not known about the affair in the servant's quarters. Steve's grim enunciation of the words "another murder" had caused the blood to ebb from her face.

But he had no intention of explaining, yet. Methodically he paced to the butler's chair and reached down to test the man's bonds, satisfying himself that they had not been loosened during the past half hour. Just where Mannix fitted into the puzzle he was not sure; but it was better to take no chances.

And it was better to take no chances on the possible return of the black-robed monster. Grimly Steve strode to the nearest of the library windows, made sure it was locked, then walked to each of the others and tested them, too. Satisfied that no intruder could enter except by the door, he locked it, put the key in his pocket, and lowered himself into a chair near the fireplace.

"There'll be some men coming from Headquarters," he said quietly. "We'll wait."

Strangely enough, neither Gloria nor the servant-woman had anything to say. For a moment it seemed that Gloria would blurt out the questions which were certainly burning on her lips, but instead she sat motionless and stared straight ahead of her, as if realizing the seriousness of the occasion. The servant-woman looked from Steve to Mannix and back again, and seemed to be striving desperately to control her emotions.

Steve volunteered nothing. His thoughts were centered on Matthew Haley and the nameless fiend who had murdered the Hungarian girl. They were not comforting thoughts. Giving voice to them would not erase that pallid expression of fear from Gloria's face, nor remove the hunted glare from the other woman's wide eyes. Silence was the best cure—silence and patience.

In the end his patience was rewarded. A bell droned in the hall, announcing the arrival of Mollison's men. He stood up, unlocked the library door, and paced down the corridor. A moment later he was giving orders to the two uniformed men who confronted him. Then he returned to the library, put both hands on Gloria Haley's arms, and said evenly:

"There's nothing to be afraid of. Mollison's men will stay with you until morning. They'll take care of Mannix, and if that other damned thing comes back to do more murder, they'll take care of that, too!"

"You—you're going to leave me, Steve?"

"I'm going to find your father."

She stared at him anxiously and reached out to hold him back. Then she regained control of herself, said in a mechanical voice: "All right, Steve," and sat motionless in her chair, watching him as he walked away.

He glanced at the clock on the mantel as he went out. The hour was one-thirty.

SIX hours later he had achieved nothing. There had been no lead to follow, nothing except the bewildering knowledge that Matthew Haley had climbed out of bed in the middle of the night and vanished.

Steve Wayne had searched the house and grounds and prowled up and down the streets of the neighborhood. He had talked to the driver of an owl cab parked near an all-night drugstore three blocks from the Haley home. But there had been no clue. Matthew Haley had simply vanished.

Now it was seven-thirty and the night was over. Wearily he made and end of his futile search and cursed himself for a fool. What had he expected? To find Haley walking the streets mumbling prayers? To find the man huddled in some obscure doorway, shivering with terror? Haley might be frightened, but

not to that extent! It was obvious now that the man had gone to some premeditated destination, perhaps to the home of a friend. But where?

Steve stood on the corner of Cypress and Verne Streets, half a mile from the Haley home, and looked both ways for a cab. A cafeteria was open on the other side of the square. He went into it, ordered coffee and a sandwich, and gulped the food without wanting it. Fifteen minutes later, suffering from fatigue and a vicious headache, he paced along the sidewalk of upper Verne Street, toward Matthew Haley's big house.

He stopped then, and stood staring at a stoop-shouldered figure shuffling across the street toward him. His eyes widened; he made a guttural sound in his throat and scowled blackly.

The stoop-shouldered figure was Matthew Haley!

For a moment Steve's astonishment paralyzed him. He gaped, unable to realize that his search was over, that it had ended precisely where it had begun—at Haley's own home. Then he advanced slowly, staring with wide eyes. Judging from the appearance of Haley's crumpled clothes and from the slow, leaden scuff of his feet as he walked, the man had spent the night in the open—had not gone to the home of a friend, after all. He looked tired, helpless. Looked as if he were suffering from a severe hangover after an all-night's drunk. And there was something wrong with one of his shoulders. It seemed abnormally large, swollen.

Steve hung back, suppressing a violent desire to stride forward and blurt out the man's name. Haley had not seen him, had not looked up. Without once turning around, he scuffed sluggishly up the cement walk of his own home and climbed the steps. He did not ring the bell, but produced a ring of keys from a pocket of his crumpled coat and fumbled with them awkwardly. When he got the door open at last, he paced over the threshold like a dead man, leaving the door open wide.

Steve followed cautiously, his eyes still clouded with bewilderment, his mouth twisted at the corners in a fixed frown. He did not understand, did not pretend to; but not once did he consider interrupting Haley's slow progress.

Wearily the man proceeded down the corridor toward the library door, looking neither to right nor left. He apparently had no intention of stopping. His destination was the staircase, and probably his own bedroom on the floor above. But the library door was half open when he came abreast of it, and before he could pace past, the door was jerked wide and Gloria Haley stepped out.

The girl stopped, rigid, gazing first at her father, then at Steve, who was pacing down the corridor not ten strides behind him. She spoke just one word—"Father!" —and spoke it in a whisper. There was no relief in her voice. Nothing but awe and amazement. She, too, did not understand.

But unlike Steve, she did not wait to see what her father would do. Her outstretched hands caught his arms, holding him, pulling him toward her. Matthew Haley looked wearily into her face and said dully, without emotion:

"What—what's the matter?"

She drew him inside, and Steve followed. A police officer—one of Mollison's men—leaned against the library table, gazing with narrowed eyes. Mannix, the butler, was asleep in his chair near the fireplace. The servant-woman was gone, probably back to her own room to get some rest now that the danger of darkness was over.

The police officer looked at Steve and said: "What's happened Mr. Wayne?" Steve said nothing, merely stared at Gloria as she forced her father into a chair and did little things to make him comfortable. Turning, she said anxiously:

"Where was he, Steve? Where did you find him?"

"I didn't."

"But—"

Steve moved forward and put both hands on Haley's shoulders, then withdrew one hand abruptly as Haley winced with pain.

"Where've you been, Mr. Haley?"

Haley looked up, mumbled thickly: "I —I don't know."

"No idea, hey?"

"I—don't remember. This house was driving me mad; I just had to get away from it. Where I went I don't know."

"You're pretty badly banged up," Steve observed. "How'd that happen?"

"I must have—fallen."

STEVE scowled suspiciously. His hand came to rest on the swollen shoulder and would have drawn aside the coat which covered it. But Haley stiffened with unexpected abruptness and dragged the probing hand away.

"It's nothing—only a bruise. Leave me alone. I'm tired. I want to go to bed and—"

Haley's head slumped down on his chest. Gloria moved toward him, stopped, and looked at Steve with a worried expression on her face.

"Do you think he's all right?" she said quickly. "Shall I call a doctor?"

"He needs sleep," Steve shrugged. "Takes a lot out of a man his age staying up all night."

Then he turned away, fearful that she might read his thoughts. They were unpleasant thoughts, caused by several significant things that refused to pass unnoticed. In the first place, that injured shoulder of Haley's needed explaining, and could not be explained away by a mere, "I must have fallen." Beneath Ha-

52

ley's coat that shoulder was bandaged heavily; and no man would have taken the trouble to wrap heavy bandages around a bruise.

Another thing: Haley was wearing shoes that did not fit him. They were not his own shoes; they were a couple of sizes too large. That, too, needed some explanation.

Steve leaned against the fireplace and stared at the man in the chair, attempting to unravel the questions and put plausible answers to them. The answers would not come from Haley himself; that was certain. Already the man was asleep, or feigning sleep. The answers would have to come from some other source. But where?

He found out a moment later. A door opened and closed in the hall, and heavy boots beat a rapid tattoo along the floor, toward the library. Turning abruptly, Steve stared into the tense face of the second of Mollison's men. The detective stood straight and stiff on the threshold, gripping the sides of the door-frame with both hands. His face was paler than it should have been. From the glare of his unblinking eyes it was evident that he had seen something not pretty to look at.

He came forward quickly and began to talk before he reached Steve's side. The words were harsh, strained indicative of overworked emotions.

"You'd better come with me, Mr. Wayne. Somethin'—well, somethin's happened. I been prowlin' around, and I took a look in the garage, and found—"

The word "garage" caused Steve to peer sharply at Matthew Haley. Especially at Haley's ill-fitting shoes. He had been trying to place those shoes, trying to decide what type of man would be apt to own them. They were fashioned of coarse-grained black leather, with solid heels and unusually thick soles.

Garage? That was enough! Trium-

phantly, Steve swung on the man from Headquarters and said: "Show me."

Then, ignoring Gloria Haley's stare, he followed the man into the corridor.

THE garage was a square cement structure about a hundred yards distance from the house proper. Striding down the gravel path, with the police officer pacing grimly at his side Steve remembered what the servant-woman had told him in the room where the girl named Olga had been murdered. Last night had been the chauffeur's night off. The housekeeper, Mrs. Pelky, had slept in the chauffeur's room, preferring its comparative isolation to the sinister threat of the Haley household.

The garage door was unlocked. Mollison's man entered, leading the way across a smooth floor, down a narrow aisle between the running-boards of two large cars which gave silent indication of Haley's financial security. A wooden stairway extended upward at the rear. The detective stood aside, allowing Steve to ascend first.

The door at the top was closed. Steve opened it, stepped quietly into the room beyond. Then he stopped abruptly and said in a low voice: "Good Lord!" And Mollison's man, entering behind him, closed the door and leaned against it, methodically lighting a cigarette.

The room was a small one, decently furnished with furniture evidently carried over from the main house. A three-quarter bed stood against one wall, a small oil-stove against another. A heavy oak table, with chairs grouped around it, loomed up in the center. In one of the chairs, stiffly upright, sat a thick-shouldered, dark-complexioned man who was evidently the chauffeur, John. And the man was a prisoner.

Ropes encircled his ankles, binding them securely to the chair-legs. Other ropes bound his arms behind him, where there was less possibility of his working them loose. Steel handcuffs held his wrists. Grimly silent, he returned Steve's bewildered gaze; and there was a challenging glint in the man's dark eyes which advertised a fiery temper behind that foreign-looking face.

But that was not all—not nearly all. Steve's gaze traveled to the bed and clung there, refusing to shift away. The bed was occupied. A woman lay there, hunched in a position of silent agony, her wide eyes gaping up at the low ceiling, her hands clenched fiercely on the crumpled bed-clothes.

She did not move when Steve paced toward her and bent over her. She could not. Her half-stripped body was stiff with rigor-mortis. Her ghastly white throat was torn horribly, just as the throats of Morgan Belzak, Mrs. Julia Ebbarton, and Olga had been torn.

The black-robed killer had claimed another victim. The woman on the bed was Mrs. Pelky, the housekeeper, and she was dead.

Steve stared down at her, unable to speak. There was no need to ask questions—not even mental ones. The monster's trademark was all too evident, and this time nothing had interrupted the fiend in his blood feast. Judging from the whiteness of the woman's body, nearly every drop of blood had been drained from it, through that hideous gash in the throat. The killer had come here after escaping from the death-room of the Hungarian girl—had come here, found Mrs. Pelky alone, and fallen upon her with the same obscene hunger which had marked his other attacks.

Who would be next?

Shuddering despite every effort to control his emotions, Steve turned to face Mollison's man and the prisoner in the chair. He understood the method of Mrs.

Pelky's death, yes, but the presence of the chauffeur was still a mystery. Obviously Mollison's man was responsible for the ropes and handcuffs—but why?

The Headquarters man answered for himself. Advancing slowly, he pulled the sodden cigarette from his lips and glared at the prisoner, then said grimly:

"That's what I found when I came in here—that woman lyin' there on the bed. It gave me the horrors I'm tellin' you, but I took a good look at her and then gave the place the once-over. Then this guy came in, kind of slow and careful like, and I figured the best thing to do was hold onto him until I could bring you over here."

The prisoner said nothing. Steve glanced at him, scowled, and said slowly:

"Why didn't you bring him to the house?"

"Well, I was goin' to. But he acted kind of hard-boiled, and I didn't want to take no chances. He's a wise guy, and the best thing to do with wise guys is put 'em in irons."

Steve stood over the prisoner's chair, stared down.

"You heard what he said. Anything to say?"

"What am I supposed to say?" the chauffeur snarled.

"Plenty, if you're wise."

"Well, I don't know what you're talkin' about, see? I was home all night and when I got back here a little while ago, this guy jumped on me. I don't know nothin' about what happened."

Steve studied the man critically, taking in every detail of his appearance from the twisted face and massive shoulders to the long, powerful legs and large feet. Perhaps the man was lying, perhaps not. There was no way of knowing yet. But the answer lay in Steve's mind, and he was becoming increasingly sure that the answer was a correct one.

"Better take him to the house." he ordered quietly. "I'll be over later."

Mollison's man nodded and set about the business of releasing the prisoner's huge body. Gun in hand, he ordered the chauffeur to stand up, then marched him to the door. Steve waited impatiently for the door to close.

Then Steve turned and made a slow, careful examination of the room, seeking something, anything, which might add to the half-formed belief in his mind. Deliberately he inspected the table, the bed, the small bureau which stood in one corner. With almost fanatical attention to detail, he picked up two pairs of shoes from beneath the bed and studied them.

Ten minutes had passed before he opened the door and descended the stairs. Even then he did not proceed at once to the house, but walked slowly around the garage, staring intently at the ground.

Then he stopped and stood motionless. At his feet, in the soft earth beneath the single window of the upstairs room, lay the deep imprint of thick-soled shoes, toes pointing inward toward the wall. The window was half open.

Someone, within the past few hours, had climbed through that window, hung at arm's length, and dropped. Unless for some unknown reason those footprints had been planted there, they had belonged certainly to the black-robed fiend who had murdered Mrs. Pelky—yet the monster had worn no shoes at all when confronted in the room of the Hungarian girl, Olga.

Steve did not know the answer. He knew only that the footprints in the ground before him were large ones, and corresponded in size to the heavy-soled shoes which lay beneath the murder-bed upstairs in the chauffeur's room.

TWO prisoners were waiting in the library when Steve returned. One of them, the chauffeur, was standing erect beside the table, staring straight ahead of him and scowling defiantly. The other, Mannix the butler, still sat near the fireplace, eyes half shut and head sunk on his chest. Matthew Haley was asleep in his chair. Gloria and the two Headquarters men looked at Steve expectantly as he entered.

There was no indecision in Steve's mind then. His plan had taken form and seemed plausible. He strode forward, glared at the chauffeur, and said grimly to Mollison's men:

"Take him to Headquarters. The charge is murder."

If the two officers were surprised, they concealed their emotions expertly. One of them tightened his grip on the chauffeur's arm and looked casually at Mannix.

"What about him?"

"I'll be responsible for him. He's just a poor fool who got himself into trouble. The chauffeur is your man."

"You'll come down to Headquarters, Mr. Wayne?"

"Later."

Mollison's men walked quietly to the door, taking their sullen prisoner with them. Mannix, leaning forward in his chair, was smiling triumphantly. Gloria Haley was staring with large eyes, as if unable to believe.

Steve a hand on Matthew Haley's shoulder and said evenly: "You hear, Haley? There's nothing more to fear."

Haley moved his head up and down wearily, too tired to be relieved.

Steve released him, said casually to Gloria: "You'd better take him upstairs," then turned to confront the butler.

Mannix peered at him intently, but said nothing.

Steve leaned against the table, waiting for Gloria and her father to leave the room. While he waited, he beat a soft tattoo on the table-top with the lean fingers of one hand. Was he being a fool?

Was he making mountains out of insignificant nothings, and charging recklessly along a road which might lead to more horror? He did not know.

He walked to the door and closed it, then returned and drew a chair close to the butler's face. Then he said grimly: "Now you're going to talk."

The butler squirmed, his lips compressed, his face red. At last he said: "You—you've no right—"

Steve leaned forward. His left hand shot out and his fingers locked on the man's shirt-front. "All the right in the world, Mannix. And enough experience in this business to make tougher birds than you warble."

The butler's Adam's apple moved up and down. His cheeks drained of color. "All—anything I may know is just—just gossip, sir. Servant's talk, as you might say. Hardly worth—"

"Out with it!"

The butler wet his lips. "It—it hurts to talk about Mr. Haley, sir. I've been with him—with his family ever since I was a shaver, and my mother before me. But they do say that back, generations ago, there was some—some *vampire* blood in his family. There!"

Steve snorted audibly, disdainfully. "Good God! Evidence, man—real evidence—is what I want." He shrugged resignedly. "All right—go ahead, then. Speak your piece!"

But though Mannix with fear in his eyes and in a hushed voice, was perfectly willing to repeat a fantastic tale of Matthew Haley's great-grandmother having been under suspicion of vampirism—"and I'd like to find any authority claiming *that's* an inherited trait," gritted Steve to himself—of any substantial light on the gruesome murders, Mannix had none.

At length, after enough cross-questioning to convince himself that the butler was either a superb liar or—and this was more likely—a badly frightened and not-too-bright servant, Steve was forced to dismiss the man.

CHAPTER SIX

In Gloria's Room

THE clock on the library mantle was striking ten that night when Steve entered the room and strolled over to turn on the radio. The day had been uneventful; he had expected it to be so. Inspector Moody had come at noon, remained to talk a while, then gone away again, sending a department car later to remove the bodies of the Hungarian girl and Mrs. Pelky. Later in the afternoon Matthew Haley had come downstairs to apologize for his actions of the preceding night.

Haley was in his study now, messing about among books and papers in an apparent effort to get his mind off the events of the past hours of horror. He little knew how close he had come to being arrested as a matter of routine—how savagely Steve had argued with Inspector Moody in a successful effort to change Moody's mind. But Moody was gone now, and the house harbored only five persons: Haley, Haley's daughter, the servant-woman, Mannix, and Steve Wayne.

Steve glanced at the clock, lowered himself into a comfortable chair, and relaxed. Relaxed physically, at least. Mentally he was living in the future. In another three or four hours, perhaps less, he would know whether or not Steve Wayne was a fool. Meanwhile, the Boston Symphony Orchestra, under the capable direction of Serge Koussevitsky, was offering Erik Satie's mournful masterpiece, *Gymnopédie*. The deep, low tones were comforting, nerve-soothing.

Steve thought of Gloria Haley, and for the first time in many hours thought of

56

her as something more than Matthew Haley's daughter. The girl was upstairs now in her own room, sleeping, with the servant-woman attendinng her. She had promised to come downstairs soon. Steve wondered if she would.

She did, even before *Gymnopédie* had reached its droning conclusion. Entering the library quietly, she came and sat close to him. She had done things to her face and hair, to erase the haggard look caused by fear and lack of sleep. She wore a dark, clinging gown which made him all the more conscious of the fact that she was a woman, and not an ordinary woman. Leaning toward him, she said quietly:

"Steve—are you really sure of yourself? Do you really believe father's chauffeur did those awful things?"

Steve scowled and stopped staring at her. Turning his head to hide the expression on his face, he answered mechanically:

"Let's forget about it."

"But—"

"It's over and done with, Gloria. I'm not over-anxious to rehash it."

He stood up and leaned over the back of her chair letting his fingers move idly through her hair. It was soft hair, unbelievably soft; and the radio in the corner was whispering one of Tschaikowsky's gentler themes in a mood not at all conducive to thoughts of murder. Steve leaned closer and turned the girl's head toward him.

"You're lovely," he said simply, and meant it.

Then he stiffened. Slow footsteps were audible in the corridor, and the doorway was suddenly full of Matthew Haley's stoop-shouldered form. Haley stared blinkingly, but did not advance across the threshold. In a thin voice he announced:

"I'm going to bed, you two. If you want to stay up, that's your own business—but you need sleep, Gloria. Do you hear?"

Gloria sighed patiently. "Yes, father."

"Good-night, then."

"Good-night."

The footsteps receded to the stairs, ascended slowly, and died out along the upper hall. Gloria sighed again and said softly: "I suppose I ought to humor him, Steve. He's been through so much."

She stood up, obviously waiting to be kissed. Steve drew her close to him and kissed her mechanically, casually. Already he was thinking of other things and wondering again if he had not made a mad mistake. When the girl left him, he stood motionless beside the library table, staring straight ahead of him and scowling. Then he strode to the radio, turned it off, and lit a cigarette.

HALF an hour later, when he paced out of the library and ascended the stairs to his own room on the upper floor, the big house was sinister with silence. A light burned in the upstairs corridor —a light which he, being the last one to retire, was supposed to turn off. He left it burning.

In his own room he turned on the lamp beside the bed, closed the door quietly, then sat on the side of the bed and drew a revolver from his pocket. Cigarette still dangling from his lips, he removed the clip from the gun, examined it, and replaced it. Then he put the weapon back in his pocket, stretched himself out at full length, and gazed moodily up at the ceiling.

Before the night was over he would know the answers to the many questions which confronted him. Of that he was certain. There was nothing to do now but wait.

Lying there he drew a mental plan of the house and its occupants. Mannix, the butler, would be asleep in his room in the servants' quarters, unless the man were a better actor than he had seemed to be while talking in the library a long while ago. The servant-woman had undoubtedly returned to the servants' quarters, too, and would be locked in her room, either sleeping or trying to. That left Matthew Haley and Gloria, both of whom occupied rooms here on the second floor of the main house. There was no one else—except the black-robed monster who came and went during the silent hours of darkness, committing horrible murder wherever his vile hands found a victim. Perhaps the man was even now a prisoner at headquarters, as Gloria and the others believed.

Perhaps not!

Steve blocked his cigarette in the bottom of an ash tray, lit another one, and looked at his watch. The hour was eleven-twenty, and the hands of the watch, as he gazed at them, moved with maddening sluggishness. Yet those hands would eventually lead to a brief interlude of hell —he was sure of it. The trap was laid. Everything now depended on patience, and on his ability to act quickly, decisively, when the moment of horror arrived.

No sound disturbed the utter stillness of the house. No sound at all. The lamp beside the bed threw a pale halo of light over the carpet, and the soft circle of illumination reached out dully to embrace the door which led to the corridor. Steve lay motionless, staring at the door, dragging deep lungfuls of cigarette smoke to keep himself alert.

Already he had blocked three butts and tossed them aside. Mechanically he shook a fourth cigarette out of its package. Then it happened.

THE sound was almost no sound at all, merely the soft, distant creaking of a door. So vague was it, and so indefinite, that it seemed to have no source, seemed to be a disembodied, ghostly whisper alive in itself, as if the silence of the big house had suddenly become possessed of a soul.

But Steve had heard it—was sure he had heard it. Cautiously he lowered both feet to the floor and stood erect, gripping the end of the bed with a rigid hand. The door seemed miles away as he stared at it; yet he knew that he must reach it and reach it without making the slightest noise. Slowly, deliberately he tiptoed toward it until his outstretched fingers curled around the knob.

He stood motionless then, every nerve alert for a repetition of the sound which had galvanized him to action. But it was not the creaking of a door that he heard; it was another sound, more significant and more sinister. Someone was moving warily, furtively along the corridor outside!

Steve's hand slid into his pocket and closed over the revolver that lay there. It was comforting, that revolver—far more comforting than the thoughts festering in his mind. He had anticipated this very thing that was happening; but reality was infinitely more vicious than anticipation. He wished suddenly that he had confided in Inspector Moody and prevailed upon Moody to remain in the house. The lone-wolf game was sometimes safer, yes—especially where silence and subtlety were needed—but if the lone wolf failed now, tonight, a woman might pay the horrible penalty for his failure!

Grimly Steve waited, listening to the rapid thumping of his own heart and the soft whisper of naked feet in the corridor beyond the door. It was a gamble. If he flung open the door and challenged the creator of those whispering footsteps, confronting the man before he could reach Gloria Haley's room, the ordeal would be over—but nothing would be proved, no questions answered. If he waited, allowing the man to reach his objective, then a single blunder on the part of Steve Wayne would be the forerunner of a tragedy unspeakable.

He waited. One hand nursed the revolver in his pocket; the other came up jerkily to wipe the cold perspiration from his forehead.

Slowly, with hellish deliberation, the footsteps whispered past his door and continued down the hall. They would never end, it seemed; but they did end. Then for a maddening interlude of uncertainty no sound at all invaded the stillness of the house. The place stopped breathing, stopped living. An eternity passed. At the very moment when Steve's nerves threatened to crack under the strain, a key grated softly in a lock, and a door opened with a single protesting groan.

Then Steve moved. Quickly, noiselessly he drew open the door in front of him and stepped into the corridor. At the far end of the passage, near the head of the wide staircase, the overhead light was still burning, casting gaunt shadows along the carpeted floor. The passage was empty. The door of Gloria Haley's room, ten yards distant, hung ajar. An hour ago—or was it longer?—that door had been closed!

Steve tiptoed toward it, every muscle tense, every nerve on edge. He had no time to think now, at least no time to think of anything but his own grim responsibility. Intuitively he knew what he would find when he invaded the girl's room, and he shuddered to think of what he might find if he were too late.

Revolver in hand, he advanced. Then he stopped. From the doorway ahead of his came a sound which stabbed into him with shocking abruptness, stifling the breath in his throat. It was a vibrant, high-pitched scream flung out of a woman's lips, and it was alive with terror.

Like the screech of a siren that scream shrilled through the corridor, smothering every other thing with its awful intensity. It ate into Steve's brain, numbing him, causing him to stand stiff and helpless for an eternity composed of endless seconds. Then the sinister sound died with uncanny quickness, as if a hand had closed over the lips that uttered it.

Steve leaped forward violently, sucking a great breath between clenched teeth. The doorway hung before him. He reached it, flung himself across the threshold, his free hand clawing at the doorframe to steady himself. His eyes were already wide open, staring. In the split-second interval that he stood swaying, his gaze swept every portion of the shadowy room, drinking in its contents.

The room was dark. But the light from the corridor, slanting through the open doorway, revealed enough to sap every trace of color from Steve's face. There was a bed, gleaming white against the wall. There was a black-robed shape bending over it, uttering guttural sounds which were half human and half animal —vile, throaty sounds of triumph and hungry anticipation. There was a woman on the bed, writhing silently and horribly in the grip of the monster's powerful hands.

Once again, as on that other occasion when he had faced the black-robed fiend, Steve gave voice to involuntary words of terror. The words welled from his throat without his knowing it. Viciously they rasped across the room.

"Stop it! For God's sake—"

The robed figure turned—turned with inhuman quickness, releasing its victim. Like a huge bat it swung about, arms upraised, eyes glaring in a face convulsed. Steve's fist jerked up, gripping the revolver. He took aim at the very center of that menacing mass. His finger tightened on the trigger.

But the finger did not tighten all the way. Staring into that white face, Steve knew that his suspicions had been correct. Like a man stricken with paralysis he stood stiff as stone, gazing into that familiar, mask-like countenance, realizing its awful significance.

Then it was too late. With a single rasping snarl of triumph, the monster was upon him.

CHAPTER SEVEN

Monster Unmasked

MADNESS took possession of Steve at that moment. Aware of his danger, he stumbled backward, both hands extended before him to hold the monster's lunging body at bay. That hideous black-robed shape was death itself, death incarnate. If it succeeded in accomplishing its purpose, the woman lying there on the bed, limp and unconscious, would be the next victim. Perhaps she was already dead. She had not moved since the fiend had released her—had not cried out or displayed any show of life.

Into Steve's mind came visions of the monster's other victims, their throats ripped open, their mutilated bodies drained of blood, their dead faces fixed in unchangeable expressions of utter horror. The visions came to him as visions might torment a man on the verge of death by drowning. He, himself, was drowning, in a vicious sea of madness. That white gargoyle of a face hung above him, inches away from his own. The wall had ended his stumbling retreat. The monster's gaunt hands were reaching toward him out of the folds of the black robe.

A gasping cry sobbed from Steve's lips. The revolver, now that it meant the difference between life and death, no longer lay in his fist. He had dropped it. Frantically he braced himself, hammered his knuckles against the face and chest of his adversary. Desperation had given him added strength. His blows drove the creature back, gave him an opening to lunge forward and hurl himself against the fiend's legs. The monster's thick-set body snapped backward, tumbled off balance, went down with a thud which shook the floor.

Steve found new life then. On hands and knees he staggered forward, hurled himself upon the black-robed shape before it could grope erect. His clenched fist rose and fell, missing its mark and thudding against the floor with an impact that drove a cruel stab of agony through his arm and shoulder. A powerful hand clutched at him, dragging him sideways. Locked in the monster's embrace, he rolled over and over, striving wildly to gain the uppermost position.

A chair stopped him. Hard, sharp timbers burned into his back with crushing force, throwing him into the full grip of the fiend's arms. For a moment dizziness overwhelmed him, leaving him limp and stunned. Then he looked into the very center of his assailant's contorted face, saw the triumph stenciled there. The killer's lips were parted, drooling; the sunken eyes were twin wells of hunger.

Instinct alone made Steve jerk his head sideways, twisting his exposed throat away from the attack of that murderous mouth. Instinct—and perhaps the subconscious memory of what had happened to the black fiend's other victims. But the drooling lips shot toward him again, intent on reaching their goal. Gaunt fingers groped up and locked in his hair, wrenching his head backward.

Steve did the only thing possible—jerked up a hand and clamped it squarely over the killer's drooling mouth. Touching that evil countenance was like touching something from the grave; it sent a chill of horror through him, loading him with nausea. But his effort brought results. The grip on his hair loosened; he heaved himself free with a violent twist of his shoulders. Once again he crashed into the legs of the table near the bed, and this time the table splintered under the impact, toppling with a crash.

Something hard rolled under his flailing arms then, something round and solid that gleamed before his eyes as it came to rest within reach of his hand. He groped for it even as the monster fell upon him with renewed vigor, snarling furiously and giving voice to enraged growls which reverberated viciously throughout the length and breadth of the death-room. The fiend would not be denied this time. His ghastly fingers raked Steve's face. His gaping mouth descended, lips apart and teeth gleaming.

STEVE'S hand closed desperately over the metal object which had fallen from the table. It was a box of some sort, probably a trinket-box in which Gloria Haley had kept feminine odds and ends. But it was a weapon now, and a last resort. It was life to a man on the threshold of hideous death.

Steve made one last lunge to escape the fiend's attack. The lunge was half successful; it carried him to his knees and left him free for the duration of a split second, swaying wildly as he sought to balance himself. His arm swung back, forward again. The base of the metal box crashed full into the killer's distorted face, as the face came closer with snake-like quickness.

The face receded, choking and gasping. Again and again Steve swung, hammering first with his naked fist, then with the knotted hand that held the blunt-edged weapon. Enormous vitality must have inhabited that black-robed body. The killer fell backward, striving vainly to seize the box in his clawing fingers. A dozen furious blows were needed to subdue him. Even then, with his gargoyle face battered almost beyond recognition, his hands and wrists gouged and bloody from the weapon's crushing impacts, he did not lose consciousness. It took a last deliberate blow of Steve's fist, delivered at close range with sledge-hammer force, to drive him to the floor and silence him forever.

But the ordeal was over then. Trembling in every muscle, Steve put both hands on the edge of the bed and dragged himself erect, to stand swaying like a man who had imbibed great quantities of liquor. A full moment passed before he found strength enough to stagger along the wall and reach out a hand to the light-switch. Then, exhausted and nauseated, his clothes torn in a score of places from the savage clawing of the fiend's fingers, he leaned against the wall and gulped great mouthfuls of breath, fighting to remain conscious.

Another full minute passed before he was sufficiently sure of himself to leave the support of the wall and stumble across the room to where his revolver lay on the carpet. He did not look down at the black-robed thing on the floor. He did not want to. He had seen enough of that hellish shape to last him a lifetime.

Slowly he moved to the bed and stared down at the motionless body of the monster's intended victim, and a sob of relief escaped from his swollen lips as he saw that the girl's throat was unmarked. He had not been too late. In another few seconds he might have been, for the girl's pajama jacket was ripped wide, exposing the entire upper portion of her body. But the killer had been interrupted before sinking his vile teeth in that ivory-white throat. Gloria Haley was unconnscious, yes—but unharmed.

The girl's eyes opened while Steve gazed down at her. They opened slowly and remained wide, her gaze focused on the bleeding wounds in his face. But she did not speak. She seemed to be struggling wearily to remember something, to gather her thoughts together and make sense of them. For a long while she lay very still, staring up at her protector; then, apparently aware of her near-nakedness for the first time, she caught the torn front of her jacket in a trembling hand and pulled it over her. And she said slowly, hesitantly:

"Steve—that horrible thing—"

Steve glanced at the thing on the floor. He could have hidden it from her, could have covered the black-robed shape with a blue blanket which lay folded at the end of the bed. But he knew better. Gloria Haley, now, was in a semistupor caused by the shock of her nightmare ordeal. Her mind was not fully receptive. It was better for her to look into that ghastly countenance now, to recognize it, rather than be denied the truth until some later time when the horror would strike her with full force.

And already the girl was staring, staring intently at the black-robed shape. Her groping hand caught Steve's arm and clung there. She said slowly:

"What—is it, Steve?"

He made no answer. Deliberately he put an arm around her and helped her to sit up. He walked with her toward the thing on the floor, and stood beside her as she gazed down into the monster's upturned face.

A HEAVY shudder passed through the girl's slender body as she looked down. Slowly, like an automaton, she sunk to her knees on the carpet, her gaze riveted immovably on those battered features.

Steve watched her intently. Would she recognize them, under that hellishly clever make-up of puttied features, of dyed gray hair and other items from the make-up box? Of course—she must!

The only sound that came from her lips was a low, tremulous moan. Stooping swiftly, Steve saw the bullet-shattered shoulder, flung a blanket over that gaunt, glaring face. Long afterward he remembered how it had looked at that second, and cursed himself for a fool for even allowing the girl to glance at it.

It glared up at that last instant, without emotion. There was no life left in it. Its sunken eyes were half-open, glazed. Its pale flesh was caked with blood, gleaming scarlet and white against the background of the carpet. Obscene hunger was still indelibly printed in those ghastly features; the bloody lips were still parted, as if eager, even in death, to fasten on the throat of some unwary victim . . .

The girl's eyes were glazing as she sank back weakly against the pillow. Steve's jaw tightened. He went to the closet, flung something over her, then went to the house phone and called Mannix.

Speaking a few words to the butler, he left—and walked slowly down the hall toward the door of Matthew Haley's room . . .

Outside he paused, listening, his hand raised against the panel. There was no perceptible sound from within. His knuckles rapped sharply.

For a long moment then, he waited.

A voice, muffled, came to him. "What is it?"

Steve went in. Matthew Haley lay on the bed; his eyes bleary, his face showing signs of suffering, of tearing nerve-straining worry.

As he saw Steve, he let out a sigh that might have been of relief.

Steve said softly: "It's happened again, Mr. Haley. For the last time."

Matthew Haley trembled as if in a fit of ague. Steve spoke soothingly, yet distinctly. "You're all right, Mr. Haley.

Quite all right now. Don't be afraid any longer. He's dead."

Haley muttered thickly, brokenly: "Are —are you—*sure?* It—it's not—I'm not the—?"

Steve smiled reassuringly. "No. I knew—I guessed—how worried you were. I found out about—about that strain that ran through your family. It is enough to frighten anyone.

There was a knock on the door. Mannix. appeared, a steaming cup of black coffee, laced with rum, on a tray. He went out immediately. Steve gave that to Haley.

"Drink it," he ordered. And then, after a moment, he spoke quietly, "Your friend—John Ebbarton—was the killer," he said.

AFTER a moment, Haley's eyes cleared. "That—hound of hell!" he gasped.

"Yes—it would be— John Ebbarton! He was a fiend—a sadist. Drove Julia from him, though God knows I was more than glad that he did—until her death. He too was suffering under a curse, though I didn't realize it at the time. Nocturnal blood-lust. He must have known it, and tried to—to kill two birds with one stone, by cleverly disguising himself as me!"

"I was sure that it was not you whom I shot in the shoulder," Steve cut in. "Though I swear I couldn't be sure at the time. His idea of killing your partner first, after you'd had that inconsequential quarrel, then—Julia. Damned clever of him to make sure that you were well hidden every time he put in an appearance."

"God man, I—I didn't know what I was doing more than half the time, except I was sure that I was living through a hell of nightmares."

Steve nodded. "When I was sure that the killer in the Hungarian girl's room wore no shoes, and then when you came home with a pair too large for you, unable to explain your absence—it sounded too good. I smelled dope on you then. I know my narcotics, and that which I smelled, I knew was not habit-forming. I suspected then that you'd been drugged without your knowledge. Had you been guilty, and smart, you'd have had an alibi.

"Ebbarton still had you in his power when he remembered that Mrs. Pelky, the housekeeper, was sleeping alone in her room over the garage. Then—after he killed her—he fed you some antidote for the drug and sent you home, dazed, after nipping you in the shoulder with a silenced gun, and putting the chauffeur's shoes on your feet."

"Yes—but the chauffeur? You were sure—?"

"He was a stall, that's all," Steve grinned. "I figured that Ebbarton might have gotten on to my true suspicions, and I accused the chauffeur of being the killer to lull any uneasiness he might have had. But I nearly let it go too far."

"How do you mean?"

"Gloria—he was in Gloria's room—"

"My God!" Haley jumped from the bed. "Is she all right?" Frantic, stark panic was in his voice as he swept blindly toward the door.

Steve nodded, took his arm. "Do you think I'd be alive if she wasn't all right," he grinned. "And now let's go to her. I think she'd like to see you—better, maybe, than she ever did before."

A smile—one of the first that Steve ever remembered seeing there—broke over Haley's thin mouth as, guided by the steadying hand of Steve Wayne, he went down the hallway.

THE END

THE COMING OF THE

*It was the soul of Hell's Courtesan
which spoke in that old bell—shrieking her midnight summons of lust and
madness to the men and maidens of Westmoorland. . . . Were all in that village condemned? . . .
Would none escape the dreadful, compelling call?
Curt Stannard prayed that the girl he loved would be
spared—and then he saw upon her white arm the brand of the
Mad Children of Satan!*

T HE bell tolled. . . . Its evil, brazen
voice struck full-throated through
the darkness. No hand that human
eye could see was plying the rope that
reached high into the ancient belfry, but
the booming tones rang a dread alarm
through the night. A moment ago there
had been peace—a waiting, dreadful hush.

MAD ONES

By Frederick C. Davis
(*Author of "She Sleeps With Murder," etc.*)

A Spine-Tingling Feature-Length Novel of Dark Mystery and Eerie Terror

. . . Now an invisible sexton from hell was belaying our ears with a fearful clangor. Slowly at first, then quickening, now swiftly, the vibrant notes beat out—pounding terror into every palpitant heart, withering the souls of all who heard.

Alone in his church, back hunched up against the altar, horrified eyes fixed on the closed doors giving onto the village green, the Reverend Matthew Middleton stood gripping a shotgun. The dinning voice of the bell shouted down upon his hoary head. The flickering light of a single candle engraved deep lines of black in his grimly determined face as he listened and watched.

The bell was tolling in the night above him, shaking the steeple at each stroke, causing the very walls to quake. A valiant man of God, he stood alone with his weapon in the dim gleam, defending his house of worship against the coming of the Mad Ones—against the coming of the Children of Satan. . . .

This I did not see, but I knew he was there, for the malignant pealing of the bell struck fear into his heart—fear as strong as the speechless terror that gripped us all.

The evil pounding pulsed into every home in Westmoorland, wringing cries of dread from women, whimpers of fright from children. Whatever they had been doing, they forgot it utterly at the first vibrant beat of the bell. Mothers gathered their young ones close, listening into the night for the sounds of running feet. Some, backed into corners by the threat that hovered all around them, stood with butcher knives clutched in their white hands. With fierce mother-love raging in their hearts they could kill—murder—rather than see their loved ones sacrificed to the hordes of the devil. For the Mad Ones were coming—coming. . . .

Nor this did I see, but I knew that in every home it was the same. Five hundred times multiplied, this scene was occurring while the evil bell tore the darkness with its convulsive voice.

THE power of the deafening clamor seemed to puff out the lights of the village. At the first swelling note, the shine had vanished from scores of windows in homes and shops. Among the first of the little stores to be plunged into blackness was that of Darrel Conger, the tobacconist. He defended himself with gloom—gloom which he hoped the Children of Satan could not penetrate to reach him with their avid hands and their thirsting teeth.

So dark was the fragrant little shop that Darrel Conger could see nothing but the dim oblongs of the windows. Quickly he passed from one to another, making sure the catches were fastened, leaving no doubt that the bolts of the doors were sunk deep in their sockets. Then, chilled with dread, hovering near his cigarette-making machine, he peered across the green at the shaking steeple of the church.

He saw the great bell swinging—the immense, heavy bell—rocking in the darkness with a fiendish violence, with a demoniacal force so strong it seemed about to tear itself from its supports. He saw the rope whipping, jerked again and again by the invisible hand of Satan, each taut pull slapping the heavy clapper. He saw this hellish frenzy of the bell, sounding its call to a carnival of sin, shrieking its summons to the Mad Disciples of the Devil. . . .

This sight lay beyond my vision tonight, but in my mind's eye I could see it, for the aged tobacconist watched each time the bell rolled out its fearful clamor— watched to see the Sons and Daughters of Satan swarm into the village.

And Dr. Humphrey Bramwell, the recluse, the enigma, the living mystery of Westmoorland—what, I asked myself, was he doing while the bell tolled? Did he pause in the midst of his strange, glittering laboratory to listen with a smile? Did he hear the wild splashing of water that signaled the invasion of the Mad Ones and say to himself, "They will not harm me, for this is my doing—mine— and I am calling them"? Did he stand in his doorway and watch for the bestial horde to appear, thinking, "I alone they will not touch, for I am their will, their master"? Did he face them fearlessly— *because he was Satan incarnate?*

I feared this man. Of this man, who was the father of the girl I loved, I was mortally afraid. I did not know what devilish wonders he performed in his secluded laboratory. There, I knew, in the dead of night, he worked with keen steel blades over dead bodies—the corpses of

66

animals, the shells of humans. Always a weird light shone in his greenish eyes. "He is mad!" I told myself each time I saw them. I was convinced of it. "He is insane!"—and I feared him.

He, too, must be listening to the bell, for the little village throbbed with its wild beating. Windows rattled in their frames under the violence of its tumult. Walls did not muffle the riotous jubilation of its vibrant voice. Minds reeled with the piercing insistence of its evil cry. It brought overwhelming fear, gnawing dread mounting with every deafening second. A singsong intonation seemed to moan beneath its cacophonous raging—a chorus lifting from the lips of the villagers—prayer.

One voice rose to defy its pervading clamor. One—a crazy shriek tearing from the throat of some man racing across the green, seeking shelter from the coming of the Mad Ones.

"Stop!" he yelled. "Stop! In the name of God, stop!"

But still the bell tolled. . . .

YOU shall learn soon what horrors the Mad Ones brought when they came. . . . But first let me take you back to an earlier hour of that same evening, to a time when the bell had yet to begin its demoniacal tolling.

We knew the danger, the two of us. We had already seen it happen. True, the bell did not raise its evil voice every night. Always, like the others in the village, we listened when the hour of twelve approached, speechless, breathless, able to think of nothing but the bell, our hearts filled with the dreadful question: "Will it ring?"

Sometimes the hour passed with the bell silent, with the village hushed in a suspense of fearful waiting. Three or four nights might follow without the clapper hammering out its devilish signal. No one knew when it would sound next. But it

would toll again eventually—of that we were certain—and the Mad Ones would come.

She came to my house just as darkness lowered. My name is Curtis Barrow. I was born in Westmoorland and, until now, spent all my years there. I am in my late twenties. Some six years ago I opened a real estate office on the green. You can easily understand that the bell, to me, was a tragedy. Once it began its infernal tolling it drove people away, began turning Westmoorland into a ruined village, abandoned and shunned.

Erica came in the evening that day. I am speaking of Erica Bramwell. As long as I can remember I have loved her. I was careful never to let her know that I feared her father. We would have been married long ago except for Dr. Humphrey Bramwell's violently unreasonable objections. Erica was loyal to her father and wished not to alienate him—most of all, she did not want to disrupt his mysterious researches to which he was devoting his every waking hour. It was a formidable barrier between us, but we knew that some day it would be overcome, that some day we would have each other, just as we always dreamed.

Erica came to me as it was growing dark. She was intensely worried. The whiteness of her flawless skin gave vivid contrast to her raven-black hair and her deep black eyes. Her red, ripe lips were trembling. For a moment, after she came in, she could not speak. She had come to me with her anxiety, I knew, because there was no one else she could turn to. At last she said:

"Curt, we've got to find Boal. Somehow we've got to find him and bring him back."

Boal Bramwell was Erica's brother—and the first to have contracted the plague of madness. He was a huge, strapping chap of powerful presence, strikingly handsome. A man whose body was as beautiful as a living Greek god's, whose soul was as vile as the pit of Hell. All his life he had seemed to court evil. His long series of escapades were a whispered scandal of the village. Looking into his malicious eyes, I had again and again suspected that he had done every foul thing man can do. I could not feel surprise that he had become one of the Children of Satan.

Perhaps you think it strange that I could detest Erica's brother so intensely, and fear her father so deeply, and yet love her with all my heart. But it is so.

A kind of madness had come upon Boal Bramwell — the madness that soon had malignantly spread to become a hellish blight upon the village. It had claimed him on a Sunday evening—on the night the bell had first tolled, after having been dug out of the earth that had hidden it for so long, and hung in the steeple of the church. The minister had rung it to summon the devout to worship. But suddenly, hearing its deep-throated call, Boal Bramwell had gone berserk. He had rushed from the house as if possessed of the devil—had plunged into the depths of the night and disappeared.

This, I thought, proved his madness. I told myself he had inherited some evil insanity from his father, that now it had broken all bounds. I thanked God that Erica had escaped the malignant strain, that she was clean of the horrible blight in the Bramwell blood.

WE could not know exactly what had happened to Boal Bramwell. We had found his car abandoned on the bank of the river, empty, with no inkling of what had become of him. Next we had heard that a girl had vanished at the same hour. Her name does not matter. She was a voluptuary with whom, I knew, Boal Bramwell had kept many a secret rendezvous. Neither returned. Theirs was the beginning of a series of baffling disappearances.

Nights later the entire village was startled out of its slumber by the sudden, mad clamor of the bell. The Reverend Matthew Middleton rushed at once to the rope, thinking it the doing of pranksters, but he found no one. The bell was tolling wildly, but no one was touching the cord! He climbed breathlessly into the steeple, to see the great, vibrating mass swinging crazily, deafeningly—and the platform empty. No one was ringing the bell, but the bell was clanging out a hellish din.

During the brazen tumult, two more disappearances occurred. One was a young man, the other a young woman, both of whom I knew. They had been seen rushing out into the night together, as though they were being driven by a delirious, irresistible impulse. As the darkness engulfed them, the tolling of the bell had ceased—only to burst out anew, as madly, the next night. During this mind-numbing turmoil of sound, three others vanished—vanished as though claimed by some lustful power so strong that the victims could not, or would not, ever to return to the world we know.

You do not understand? Why did this happen, you ask, and where did these unfortunates go? What drove them from their homes and trapped them afield? It is impossible to answer these questions clearly. I can only tell you of the frightful doubt that assailed us, of the cold terror that crept into our hearts with the haunting wonder of who will be next? . . . Who will be next? . . .

Then the Mad Ones came. The Mad Ones were those who had been missing. They came as the bell tolled. As the brazen tongue beat out its call, they swarmed into the village. They ran with the swiftness of jungle savages. They appeared in the light, half clothed, some of them, others nude. I saw them myself, their bodies wet with some sort of foul slime. Their eyes were wild. They uttered shrill, hungry cries. Their teeth gleamed. They came from everywhere.

I saw them hurl themselves upon their victims. I saw young men and women clutched in their muddy hands and dragged off into the darkness. Others I saw who had, somehow, managed to escape them. Two girls I remember, and a young man, their clothing ripped away, their arms, shoulders and necks covered with the red indentations of human teeth. The bites of the Mad Ones had drawn blood. The fangs of the Mad Ones had opened their flesh.

And then, when next the bell tolled, those who had been bitten rushed, in an orgiastic ecstasy, to join the Children of Satan, to disappear into the night, to colony themselves in some evil, hidden Eden.

Merciful God! This is a contagious madness, we told ourselves. This is some plague of insanity borne on the hungry teeth of the crazed! Those who are bitten are poisoned with evil, doomed to become like the beasts who bit them.

They had swarmed into the village again and again. Each time the bell tolled their coming. Each time they snared new victims, left the marks of their fangs in the flesh of those they trapped. On each fearful occasion the bell ceased its wild clangor as the raid culminated in a barbaric rush back into the depths of the night. Medical ministrations could do nothing for those marked with the teeth of the Mad Ones. We saw the madness possess them, more strongly as each hour passed, before our very eyes.

Erica had come to me to speak of Boal. It was he, we all knew, who was the favorite son of Satan. We had glimpsed him, almost naked, rushing through the dim light of the moon, teeth bared. We

had tried desperately to capture him, but with his animal-like sagacity he had outwitted us, with his overpowering strength he had broken out of our grasp. Fear of being bitten with his poisonous teeth had hampered us in our attempt. Yet, we all realized that unless he was taken, his venom would spread until its corruption doomed us all.

"We've got to find Boal," Erica had said. "Somehow we've got to find him and bring him back."

More to satisfy her anguish than in hope of succeeding, I answered at once: "I'll do my best. Possibly the most likely place to look is in the woods along the river." A squad of State Troopers, I knew, had already searched that section, without result, yet it was the most promising possibility. "Stay here, Erica," I urged. "It's too dangerous for you to go—"

She insisted: "I'm coming with you. Please don't ask me to stay back, Curt— I *must* go. If we should find Boal, he'll listen to me, if to no one else. Let's hurry."

Just as we were leaving the house, a car pulled up. Stephen Heath was at the wheel, and Faith Atwood was with him. Steve was my closest friend. Friendship is really too weak a word for the bond that existed between us four. We had been together longer than we could remember—Steve always with Faith, I always with Erica. He was clean-cut, thoroughly splendid, a brilliant young attorney. Faith was blonde, warm, lovely. They made an ideal pair, devotedly and mutually in love. I told them quietly:

"We're going to look for Boal."

THEY insisted on coming with us. We used Steve's car, a sedan. He drove. At first, trying to cover our misgivings, we kept up a continual bantering conversation. It was an ineffectual attempt—soon we grew silent. We said nothing whatever as we followed the dirt road which wound through the woods along the river. It was oppressively dark, with only the wavering shafts of the headlamps cutting through the gloom. Proceeding slowly, we searched the shadows.

Steve, I knew, was carrying a revolver. I had an automatic in my hip pocket.

We realized it was a hopeless search, but we persisted. We scanned every road, every path, because Erica's anxiety would not permit us to leave a single possibility untouched. She resolutely fought back the tears welling into her eyes. It was an interminable ordeal, fraught with fear, that hunt through the woods, yet we kept at it doggedly. We saw nothing. At last Steve said quietly:

"We have just time to get back to the house before twelve."

We started toward the village—started, but abruptly stopped. A snapping sound startled us. It had come from the hood. The car rolled on a few feet, but the compression of the motor, no longer firing, dragged us to a standstill. I heard Erica's breath catch. Faith's fingers rose trembling to her lips. Steve gazed at me an instant, horror glinting in his eyes. Suddenly he and I, at the same moment, dove out of the car.

We flung up the hood and searched for the trouble — searched in vain. There seemed to be nothing amiss. We quickly checked the ignition wires, made sure the gas line was not clogged, then scrambled back in. The starter growled under Steve's foot, but the engine would not catch. He tried again and again, then stopped, lips pressed.

"We've got to make a run for it," he said.

We hurried Erica and Faith out of their seats. Gripping their arms, we ran along the road. I glanced at my strap-watch as the glow of the headlamps dimmed behind us. It lacked only a few minutes of midnight. We ran faster. We stumbled breathlessly along a road so dark we could hardly see it. Cold fear filled us. When it seemed we could run no farther, we kept running. We came within sight, at last, of the village lights.

Then the bell began to toll.

We flung ourselves through the gloom with the pealing of the bell driving us like a whip of terror. At first we heard a splashing of water. Then we sensed incredibly quick movements in the darkness. We caught the padding of running bare feet. We heard quavering shouts, shrill cries. They were coming—the Mad Ones. They were swarming out of the night, closing upon us. The vile-fanged Children of Satan. . . .

BEFORE our eyes the lights of the village blinked out. We ran wildly along the edge of the green, seeing white faces dimly outlined in the windows— terrified women and men watching for the coming of the Mad Ones. No door we passed, we knew, would open to admit us. No reassurance we could shout, no plea we could utter, would draw the bolts which had been fastened against the mad horde. The clamor of the bell was too deafening, the terror of the self-imprisoned too great.

The Mad Ones mobbed through the gloom like a pillaging savage tribe, while we raced to the door of my house. Glancing back, we could see them faintly in the star-shine—naked, slime-smeared bodies, bared teeth gleaming. They were close behind us now—horribly close. We flung ourselves toward my door, desperate in our exhaustion—but too late. They rushed us, screaming madly.

Steve and I spun about, our guns in our hands. We did not wish to kill. We knew many of these people who had become human devils. Crazed as they were, we could not drive bullets into some who had been our friends. We whipped out our weapons like steel lashes. Steve saw avid hands fastened upon Faith—muddy, lustful hands. He hurled himself into a frantic attempt to beat back the naked man. My gun cracked against the bare shoulder of a girl whose hands were stretching for my throat, whose teeth were bared. I struck her away while thrusting Erica inward through the door. Hunger for flesh—I saw it in glaring eyes and open mouths.

Steve tore Faith free, placed himself in front of her, struck out with gun and fist. We straddled, fighting a howling, reeking demoniacal horde. Hands reached, grappling. Teeth snapped at our flesh. We struggled shoulder to shoulder in a blood-chilling nightmare of swarming, hellish fiends. Suddenly, without knowing quite how we achieved it, Steve and I found ourselves on the inside of the door, the bolt driven into its socket.

We were breathless, stunned with exhaustion. He hurried to Faith and Erica, listening to the turmoil of the Mad Ones wailing around the house. They were seeking a way in. Their fists hammered the windowpanes, their shoulders crashed against the doors. Then, with the fury of the demented, they abandoned us, and shrieked away in search of easier prey. We heard them scattering across the green, their lustful voices mingling with the evil clangor of the bell.

Faith Atwood was standing rigid in the light. Our stinging eyes turned to her—to her hand, extended, trembling. In the horror of that moment we could speak no word. The frightfulness of the thing we saw held us transfixed. For there was blood pooled in Faith's palm — blood trickling from a curved wound in the fleshy part of her hand. The marks of teeth!

The poisonous bite of a human demon!

CHAPTER TWO

Captives of Madness

THEY were gone. . . .

The bell had ceased its wild ringing. Its surging vibrations had quavered off into a fateful hush. As swiftly as they had swept down upon us, the Mad Ones had rushed away. They had, we knew, seized more victims. Their malignant teeth had marked others with the virus of a bestial insanity. But we—the four of us, sheltered in my house, behind bolted doors and barred windows—gave no thought to the others. Our hearts were filled with compassionate pity for Faith.

Utter despair dulled her eyes. They seemed to say, "It is all over for me. I am lost. Nothing you can do will help me now. Soon the animal madness will claim me." She tried to force a smile, but we could not answer it. She wrapped her handkerchief about her hand, and sat on the couch. Her glance around meant that she wanted a cigarette. I gave her one from my case. She drew deeply on it while we were dazedly silent. At last, in a whisper, she asked:

"How long? How long before—"

We could not answer her. Her fingers sought Steve's yearningly and clung tightly. She did not want to leave him. Whether by death, or by madness, she did not want anything to separate her from him. She trembled a little, smoking the cigarette very rapidly, and said, quietly:

"These are very good cigarettes, aren't they?"

She was speaking of trifles because she could not voice her exquisite anguish. Darrel Conger's cigarettes? He was one of my clients, so I always bought my smokes from him. They somehow had a lulling fragrance that we could find nowhere else. He was kept busy supplying the village, often mixing blends to order—mine among them. There was Faith, sitting on my couch, speaking of such a trifle as a cigarette, when the doom of Hell itself was upon her.

Suddenly Steve tore his fingers from hers. He ran from the house. We did not know what urgency was driving him. While he was gone, I determined to do what I could for Faith. I brought a basin of hot water, made thick suds, and washed her wound. I poured antiseptic into the tooth-marks. She did not even wince at the sting. I bound a bandage over it. It was not until I had finished that she said, with a sweet and gentle smile:

"It's no use, Curt."

Steve hurried back. The shaggy-headed, hunch-shouldered man who followed him in, carrying a medical case, was Erica's father, Dr. Humphrey Bramwell. Demon he might be, but with all that he was a skilled surgeon, a physician of long experience. I drew back, scrutinizing him sharply while he bared Faith's wound and examined it. Crazy thoughts raced through my mind, but I did not speak.

Look upon your work, Satan! See the mark of your evilness upon this girl! Witness the virulence of your pestilence changing her before our eyes, poisoning her every vein and every organ. Look upon a lovely young woman whom your blight soon will turn into a barbaric she-devil. This is your doing—Satan incarnate!

Dr. Bramwell's huge head wagged. He had opened his case to minister to Faith, but now he closed it. His shoulders drooped. He said in a low, whispering rumble:

"Poor child. . . . poor child."

WITHOUT another word he left Faith. Steve, in his desperation, was not content with that. He hurried after the doctor. I could hear them talking on the porch, Steve demanding to know the truth, the physician declaring that no known treatment would allay the blight that had fastened upon Faith. She too heard. Her face became deathly white. She said nothing, but I knew she was wondering, *How long? . . . How long?*

I hurried out to Steve to find Dr. Bramwell trudging across the green. Steve was staring fiercely after him. Steve's fists were clenched, his eyes blazing. He burst out vehemently:

"What is that man? In God's name, what is he? Is his son the source of this horrible madness. Have you ever heard him speak the slightest concern for Boal? Have you ever seen him so much as lift a finger to bring Boal back? No! Merciful God, Curt, what has he done? What vileness is it that's come out of his laboratory —that place full of serums and toxins and dead organs? Is it running wild, contaminating all of us, because he wishes it to?"

I urged: "Be careful of what you say, Steve. Someone is listening."

"Let them listen!" The words rang from his lips. "Let them hear the truth! There in that laboratory of his—what devilish experiments does he perform? I've heard him say—heard him myself, several times—say how much he needs human specimens for his researches. His own son! God above, did he deliberately inoculate Boal with some serum that has caused this plague? He's not human! He's a fiend—a fiend!"

There were listeners. I saw them on the sidewalk, dark figures, pausing alert. They were men and women who had ventured from their homes, perhaps in search of loved ones who were missing—daughters and sons seized upon by the Mad Ones and dragged away. I heard their breath quicken, saw their eyes flash with fear. I saw them stare toward the laboratory of Dr. Bramwell. One of them exclaimed:

"It's true! This is his doing. That place is Satan's house. We'll never be free until we get rid of him. I say run him back into hell, where he came from! I say burn that damned place down! If we don't, he'll turn us all into obscene animals—every one of us!"

They hurried away. I looked about. Lights were reappearing in the windows. No eye had closed in sleep before the bell had raised its fearful voice, and now the pervading dread was even stronger. I saw men and women hurrying from their doors, keeping their children close, carrying suitcases, dragging trunks onto their porches. Cars were taken from the garages and loaded with homely possessions. All over the village this was happening—the beginning of an exodus from a blighted land.

We hurried back to Faith. She was sitting as before, smoking a cigarette, trying to smile. Steve took her in his arms, held her yearningly, pressed his face into her hair. Erica turned away. It hurt my eyes. How horrible to feel that we could do nothing! This splendid, young, warm, radiant girl soon inexorably to be claimed by a doom more frightful than mere death. We could not leave her. We stayed near her, during an interminable period of ghastly waiting—waiting for the madness to take her. . . .

I looked out the window as the darkness of night began to pass. Strange, I thought.

The villagers who had abandoned their homes were now returning. The heavily loaded automobiles that had paraded out of town in the dark were coming back. It was as though they had met some insuperable obstacle on the road that had forced them to abandon their plan of escape. I saw abject despair in their faces, utterly hopelessness, craven fear.

Why, I wondered, were they returning? What force had obliged them to retreat to inevitable, frightful doom? Then, soon, I learned. We all learned.

WITH the dawn came the tramping of martial feet. The steady, heavy tread opened the eyes of many who were fearfully sleeping. It brought to many windows the faces of those who had dared not look out all during the long night, even after the horde of the Mad Ones had fled. It opened doors to the first light of a new day—a day that would promise only a greater horror.

The uniformed column marched smartly to the center of the green. A commanding officer halted it with a ringing shout. He waited while men and women straggled from the surrounding homes and stores. Curiously, hopefully, I mingled with them. I saw, in the forefront of the gathering crowd, the haggardly benign features of the Reverend Matthew Middleton, and the loose-jowled face of Darrel Conger, the tobacconist. From his porch, I noted, Daniel Warlaw watched—a bald old man for many years confined to a wheel-chair, the most venerable of all the village inhabitants.

The officer snapped a document from his pocket and read. We were too startled to catch more than a phrase here and there. The hope we at first felt soon gave way to a hushed and bewildered apprehension.

"By order of the power vested in me as Governor I do declare the village of Westmoorland to be hereby placed under martial law. It is my purpose that the citizenry of Westmoorland shall be protected, the peace of their homes preserved, under the guardianship of the State. By voluntarily requesting this action, the selectmen of Westmoorland have placed the village under the orders of Captain Delevan, in command.

"It is further declared that the entire village of Westmoorland shall be closed until further notice under a condition of strict quarantine. The inhabitants of Westmoorland are herewith forbidden to pass beyond its limits. It is further rigidly stipulated that no person may enter the village of Westmoorland except when empowered to do so with a pass issued by the State Director of Health. Violation of these regulations will be drastically dealt with and offenders severely punished by imprisonment."

Captain Delevan snapped an order. He advanced to the bulletin board affixed to the front of our modest town hall and thumb-tacked the declaration of emergency upon it for all to read. His men quickly scattered around the green and into the streets. They took strategic positions and at once began their patrols, rifles glittering on their shoulders. At this I heard hollow laughter.

"Do they think bullets can stop the devil? Do they think they can scare Satan himself?"

Satan himself! Is he here, I asked myself, to witness this threat to his fiendish supremacy? Has he come from his hellish brews in his laboratory in the person of Dr. Humphrey Bramwell to hear this challenge? It is he, I wanted to shout— he whose work this is! He whose power is turning men and women into beasts! He who loosed the infectious evil—Satan himself!

From the steps of the town hall, the crusty Captain Delevan gruffly answered the questions of the crowd. Provisions, he declared. must be brought from outside to the town line and there left, to be picked up later by the tradesmen. Incoming mail would be treated in the same manner, while outgoing mail would cease to flow. Communication by wire remained—that was all. All direct intercourse between Westmoorland and the outer world had now ceased. The village had become an isolated hell.

I RETURNED to my house. Erica and Steve and Faith were still there. Faith's father and mother had died years ago; her home was a small apartment on the other side of the village; but she had not wished to go to it. She wanted to stay with Steve, because the time was short. She stifled her mounting anguish. The only indication of it was the many cigarettes she smoked to ease her shrieking nerves. And we could see, as the day progressed; the madness coming upon her.

It shone in the wildly ecstatic gleam of her eyes, in the lustful working of her red lips—pagan desires pervading her.

Darkness came. Darkness, and with it the imminence of midnight, the hour of evil. Each ticking minute goaded us. Each passing hour whipped us with a growing frenzy which we dared not reveal. The relentless clock mocked us. With doomful slowness its hands snipped off the intervals of time. It was nearing midnight now. Midnight, when the Mad Ones. . . .

We had been nervously silent. We had found no words to utter. We had kept the hush helplessly while the plague grew stronger in Faith's hot veins. Suddenly, startling us, she leaped up to fling her arms crushingly tight around Steve.

"Don't let them take me! When they come, keep them from me! Don't let me become one of them! Anything, darling —do anything to stop me! Lock me up— beat me—even kill me! But don't—*don't let them take me!*"

This while we waited, dreadfully wondering, if tonight the bell would toll. . . .

* * *

I will tell you now of the bell.

Not, as far back as we could remember —except Daniel Warlaw, the invalid confined to a wheelchair and the eldest in the village—not within our memories had there been a bell in the steeple of the church. Its emptiness was a fact we had all accepted as a matter of course. We knew, of course, that other villages summoned worshippers to service in the House of God with a reverent tolling, but this had not happened, as long as we could recall, in Westmoorland. Our church had no bell; this was so, and no one thought to change it until, by chance, the existence of the great bell was discovered.

Just before the Reverend Matthew Middleton answered his call to Westmoorland, Darrel Conger, tidying the library in the rectory, had come upon a book of old church records. The pages were yellowed and flaking away, the writing faded and almost illegible. Poring over these ancient inscriptions night after night, steeped in the fragrance of the tobacco and the herbs in his shop, Conger had painstakingly deciphered them. He had found strange mention of a bell having been taken from the steeple and buried in the churchyard. Curiously, noting the recorded spot, he had dug. Having told of his purpose, other men aided him. Soon their spades and shovels struck hard, resonant metal. Before long they had completely uncovered the bell. Then it was that the first strange thing was noticed. Long as the bell had remained interred in that rich, black soil, it had not rusted. It was as bright, as smooth, as untouched by corrosion as the day it was cast.

Inspecting it, the townsmen had found an inscription on it stating that it had been made in Westmoorland, at a forge which long since had ceased to exist. This, the Reverend Middleton declared was the bell which belonged in the empty church steeple, which had long ago sounded its call to the devout. We considered it a precious find and decided, of course, it must be returned to the belfry. Again its voice must lift across the village.

It was Daniel Warlaw, the oldest man in Westmoorland, who, hearing of the discovery, had wheeled himself agitatedly across the green to shriek at us that to sound the bell would call into the church —not the worshipful—but Satan himself.

We did not laugh at him openly, but naturally we were scornful. We persisted in the task of raising the bell from its bed of loam and mounting it in the steeple where, we considered, it belonged—persisted even after we heard his breathless story.

This is the story Daniel Warlaw told:

The forge sat on the bank of the river in those days, when the village was merely a cluster of small homes about the church, whose steeple lifted its cross above the crests of the surrounding hills. At night the chimney of the forge flared flame and sparks as though the forces of hell were pouring up through the crust of the earth. No one knew, then, the truth about John

Mortus, the iron worker. It was he who had cast the bell.

He had labored on it day and night, the task making him a recluse. He had promised the congregation as fine a bell as could be wrought, one whose powerful voice could never be forgotten once it smote the ears. He had worked in secret, wishing no eye to behold it until it was polished, the final loving touches having perfected it. And at last he had revealed the bell in all its brazen glory, and it had been hung in the steeple.

All this time we had wondered (Daniel Warlaw told us) about the vanishing of the woman. She was a creature of evil. She was a tempter of men, a hungerer after flesh. She was shunned by all the good of the village. Wickedness lived in her—a joyful evilness that knew no wrong. A fit mate, they said, for Satan himself, for hers was a lustfulness that devoured the very souls of those she took in evil communion. Somehow, after a time, she was seen no more.

I recall (Daniel Warlaw told us) the first Sunday the great bell tolled. Its sonorous tones reverberated through the clear sunshine of the morning. The devout came. They gathered in the pews. They bent their heads in prayer while the resonance of the bell still pervaded the solemn air. Suddenly a startling, soul-chilling cry rang through the church. Every eye lifted to the wild-eyed man who had shouted—John Mortus, the maker of the bell.

"Listen!" he shrieked. "She is calling! It is her voice you hear! She is crying for her mate—the devil! Hear her sobbing out her yearning! Hear her moaning her passion for him! It is not a bell you hear —it is Lucifer's woman! She is the bell! *She is the bell!*"

HE fled screaming from the church. Never again was he seen. Some said

he flung himself into the fires of his forge, that his ashes mingled with the ashes on his hearth. It is enough to know that he had confessed a hellish love, this man who had made the bell. Dismayed as we were, we climbed the steeple to look at it. We found, examing it, that it was not, as we had thought, perfect. We detected one flaw—a white spot—something embedded in the congealed metal.

It was a bone. A human bone. Part of the skeleton of the woman of evil whose flesh had not quite been consumed in the molten metal before it was poured. The blood and body of Satan's mistress were imprisoned in the bell—and its voice was her voice, crying for her mate in hell!

That was why the bell was taken from the steeple (the old man said). Because its tone carried a spell of lust. Because it stirred craven souls with thoughts of the woman and drove them to violate the commandments. Because it defiled the House of God and put a pestilence of sin into the very air. So they had taken the bell down from the steeple, and dug a hole for it in the earth in order that the voice of Satan's mate should never again be heard.

Then, while the rich, black dirt lay open to receive the bell (the ancient went on) Satan himself struck out his wrath. So suddenly it happened, no man knew the wherefore of it. One moment they had been heaping loam into the hollow to cover the bell. The next moment, following a flash and an angry roar, a ball of fire had thundered up. The blaze leaped high, radiating withering heat, flinging red tongues up to endanger the church itself.

This is no legend (Daniel Warlaw insisted) because with these eyes I saw it happen. I saw the fire leap up out of the earth like the anger of Satan himself. For moments we were so stunned no man could move. Then, seeing that the house of worship was endangered, we hastily shoveled earth into the fire. We scooped it up in

76

frantic haste, not only cutting down the heaps we had excavated, but bringing more in barrows and wagons. We were so full of fear, our only thought was to cover the bell, to stamp out the flame, to quench this display of Satan's wrath.

Perhaps we were too full of dread to think aright, but we persisted in heaping dry earth upon the bed of the bell until a huge mound grew. In truth, we created a small hill over the spot where the bell lay buried. We snuffed out the flames, but even though we labored long, the fumes seeped up through the dirt, the smouldering of hell filled the air with fetid smoke. We could not stop (the old man said) until the bell was buried so deep that the flames were smothered out and the faintest wraith of fumes was gone.

The years have worn down that hill, as they have worn our memories. Now again the rich, black earth lies open, and the bell is exposed—still bright, still shining, still free of rust. This is not a bell you have found (Daniel Warlaw declared). It is the black soul of the mistress of Satan.

Now you are giving her tongue. Now you are opening her throat so that she may cry out to Satan. And Satan will come. . . . will come. . . .

This is the story of the bell which the old man told us while we scoffed.

* * *

Midnight was near.

Faith Atwood clung desperately in the arms of the man she loved. Her plea had cut to our very hearts. "Don't let them take me!" She had sobbed it again and again. Steve Heath drew back from her, his eyes anguished, his lips hard set. He circled the room, making sure the windows were fastened, the doors bolted. Then, taking a key, he signaled me to the entrance and warned Erica:

"Stay with her. Don't let her out of your sight an instant. We will be back soon—after midnight."

We hurried out. Steve did not speak. Striding side by side, we cut across the green to the entrance of the church. A faint glimmer was shining through the colored glass of the windows—a single candle burning on the altar. We found the side door locked. We rapped and rapped again before the Reverend Matthew Middleton opened the door a crack to peer out with one watery, haggard eye.

We thrust in without speaking. Steve at once opened the door leading to the belfry. He climbed up through a trap, I following, until we stood on the platform, with the darkness around us, the night wind soughing. There the bell hung. Its weighty mass inert, it was a gleaming shadow in the darkness. Steve, his eyes narrowed, struck a match and bent close.

There, in the metal, was the white spot —the bit of bone visible through a flaw— all that was left of the body and the blood of Satan's woman.

My strap-watch read one minute of midnight.

Thirty seconds.

Ten.

The hour.

A BRAZEN voice struck out of the bell. Suddenly its tone beat deafeningly into our ears. It had not moved, but the clapper had swung. A single stunning blow sent vibrations shivering around the metallic lips. Then another, and another —quickening, faster, faster! The impacts of the clapper made the bell itself swing. Its fiendish cry swelled out.

Steve Heath flung himself upon it. He reached for the hammer and gripped it, but some diabolical force, stronger than his strength, tore it from his fingers. It beat, beat, beat. Desperately, crazily, Steve fastened his arms around the bell. With his body he tried to stifle its pulsant roaring. He was lifted from his feet, tossed back and forth. He could not retain his grip. It hurled him down.

The bell tolled wildly—the woman of evil shrieking to Satan—summoning the children of Satan. . . .

Steve dragged himself up, dazed, gasping. He heaved himself upon the bell again. This time I fought it from the opposite side. It was useless. The diabolical power of the bell overwhelmed us. It flung us back and forth, crushing our ribs, striking the breath from our lungs. We were mad, I think—mad, up there in the belfry, fighting that evil monstrosity of metal. Mad because we thought we might choke off its malignant voice—but we could not.

Suddenly Steve tottered away. He stumbled down the narrow stairs. I followed him closely. As we sped to the door the minister hurried after us to bolt it, his shotgun gripped in one blue-veined hand. We heard the bolt click into its socket behind us. We ran across the green as fast as our legs could swing—ran crazily, because we heard the Mad Ones swarming into the village.

They were rushing through the darkness. They were darting from shadows, their naked, slimy bodies flashing, their bared teeth gleaming. We raced ahead of them to my door. They were closing in from everywhere when we stumbled breathless upon my porch. We tensed to thrust through, but froze, peering back, for at that moment a ringing, commanding voice shouted through the dinning of the bell.

"Pick them off!"

It was a shouted order of Captain Delevan. We glimpsed him, standing on the roof of the tobacconist shop, his stocky figure outlined against the starry sky. Swift glances around showed us other figures posted in lofty places. Militiamen were staring out of upper windows, brac-ing against chimneys, rifles in their hands. And then, as the evil shadows of the Mad Ones darted across the green, the weapons barked.

"Pick them off!"

Screams shrilled out of the night. I saw a naked girl fall with crimson streaming down across her breasts. I saw a nude man stumble to his knees with scarlet spurting from his forehead. Whining bullets were protecting us from the pestilence of the disciples of the King of Hell. More than this, Steve Heath did not wait to see, for his anxiety for Faith was a driving obsession. We flung ourselves into the house and bolted the door while the rifles whipped death upon the Mad Ones.

We stopped short in the living room. My eyes fastened upon Erica. Her clothing was half ripped from her body. Her whole being was quaking with insupportable dread. She was retreating across the room—retreating from a horror. That horror was Faith Atwood. Faith's eyes were blazing fiendishly. Her hands were raised to claw. And her teeth were bared —bared and shining hungrily.

"Faith!" Steve shouted. "In God's name —Faith!"

She whirled on him. He tried to catch her in his arms. He was risking the venom of her fangs, but in his unreasoning anxiety he was thinking only of the girl he loved —this she-fiend. She tore away from him at once, with terrible strength. She cried out savagely:

"I am going with them! I am one of them! I am their kind! They are calling for me—calling!"

The bell was tolling wildly.

She flung herself from Steve. His strength was not enough to hold her back. Every foot of the way to the entrance he grappled with her, but he could not stop her. She pulled the bolt free. She wrenched herself from Steve's grasp and flung herself out. She raced into the darkness—raced out onto the green where bullets were whining, where the air was churning with the beating of the bell, where the Mad Ones were swirling in their obscene dance of capture.

Steve ran after her. Unmindful of the rifles, he sought her in the darkness. "Faith! *Faith!*" as she engulfed herself in the tumult she tore her clothing from her body. Her course was marked by the shreds of her garments. Blindly Steve searched for her while the tolling of the bell began to slow down, while the Children of Satan swarmed back into their secret hell with their captives—among them the girl Steve loved.

CHAPTER THREE

Citizens of Hell

WITH my automatic in my hand, I stood at the door, bracing it with my foot, staring until Steve vanished in the gloom. Then I turned back quickly. I found Erica standing where I had last seen her, trembling, her face streaked with tears. I seized her hands. I said quickly:

"I've got to go after Steve. He's alone out there. If I don't, he may never come back. They're gone now, Erica, but we can never be sure. Somehow, while I'm gone—" My aching eyes roved the room. "I'm going to lock you up. There's no other way. I can't take you home—not now. I've got—to lock you up."

Take Erica home! The thought chilled me. Take her home to place her under the custody of Satan? What devilish thing did her father do to his son? What horrible thing might her father do to his daughter? Demon that he is, will he hesitate to inflict the blight of the evil madness upon her? This I asked myself even while the impossibility of the thought of taking Erica home repelled me. I could not surrender her to the house of Satan.

I opened a closet in the corner of the room. I gripped Erica's arms and forced her into it. I closed the door upon her, twisted the key in the lock, then slipped it into my pocket. She was a prisoner in a stiflingly confined space. She did not protest. No sound came from beyond the door. She knew, as I knew, that it was best this way—until we were sure all the Mad Ones had fled.

I would kill her, I thought, rather than let the demons claim her. I would send a bullet through the heart of this girl I loved rather than lose her to the obscene fiends who hunger for her. It would not be murder, I told myself, but mercy. My bullet, if it came to that, will save her from the carnal embrace of Satan.

I hurried from the house. Now lights were reappearing in the windows. In the gleam I saw the sentries still posted, alert with their rifles, still ready to tear down any of the Mad Ones who appeared. The darkness was in turmoil with men and women rushing from their homes. On the green, dead, naked bodies were lying—the tooth-marked Children of Satan—naked and slimy. And out of the gloom came a steady, rhythmic pounding.

I saw a man—one who, until the coming of the Mad Ones, had been a staid and conventional tradesman—a man kneeling over the naked body of a girl, a sharp-pointed wooden stake in one hand a heavy hammer in the other. He was driving the pin through her dead heart. He was pinioning her to the green in a pool of her defiled blood. I turned away, too sick at heart even to feel sick, for I recognized this man and this girl. She, I knew, was his daughter.

"Now she is dead!" he cried out. "Now she is dead. . . . dead. . . . dead!"

And cries came out of the darkness. "Burn them! Burn their evil flesh! Make sure that Satan will not bring them back

79

to life! Save them from him. Burn them!"

Flames began to flicker—matches licking their fire into gathered twigs—as I raced out of the village. I was seeking Steve Heath. In all that wilderness of darkness I did not know where he had gone, but I knew that the Mad Ones always fled toward the river. I hurried along a dark path and came to the soft bank. Peering through the gloom, I saw a figure standing motionless, silhouetted against the faint rippling of the water. I drifted toward it. It was Steve.

"They've gone across to the island," he told me. "All of them—on the island. Faith is with them. God above, I can't let them keep her there!"

I STARED at the mound of shadows looming across the water. It was a nameless island, high-crowned, craggy, covered with lush vegetation. Steep-banked as it was, covered with odorous jungle growths, it had been allowed to remain untouched. Tonight it looked as silent, dark and deserted as ever, though a strange pall seemed to be floating over it—a ghostly, hovering cloud. It was, I realized at once, an appropriate lair for the Mad Ones, that evil Eden.

Steve began throwing off his clothing.

He kicked off his shoes, stripped himself until he stood almost naked. I stood dumbfounded a moment, then seized his firm arm. He scarcely seemed to heed me, but stared across the dark water at the sinister island with the almost invisible black cloud floating over it.

"In God's name, what are you going to do?" I demanded. "Don't you realize what a risk it is—going over there? You may never come back. You'll be one against a horde. Listen to me, Steve! You don't dare—"

"I'm going to Faith."

He said it so quietly, so firmly, I knew that argument was useless. He started down the bank toward the water. I kept hold of his arm. "In that case," I said. "I'm going with you."

I threw off my clothes rapidly as he went on. Quietly he crept into the water, looking always at the island. I hurried after him, lowered myself from the bank. The river was cloyingly warm and, I knew, blackened with silt stirred up by the passage of the Mad Ones. Together we struck out. We swam with quick, quiet strokes toward the island.

In the shadow of a rocky ledge we trod water, searching for a way onto that isolated, ominous circle of land. We heard voices carrying on the wind—a low, sing-song chant, rising from many throats in barbaric chorus. As we found a cleft and climbed up, the mad music grew louder in our ears. We paused on the ledge, our bodies dripping turgid water, aware that we were now enveloped in a strange, haunting fragrance.

It was a penetrating, exalting incense that flowed around us in the night air—a faint fog that grew thicker as we groped our way toward the center of the island. Thorns ripped at us, trailing vines clung to us, but we were aware chiefly of the mono-tone of voices and the thickening mist that enwrapped us. It was a low-floating body of smoke drifting from some hidden point in the midst of the primitive jungle. It permeated everything—even, we thought, our brains and our flesh and our souls. . . .

We crept along a descending path, be-tween rearing, jutted walls. Each step downward thickened the viscid smoke. Breathing of it, I felt a strange exaltation, a kind of ecstasy. I knew, too, that Steve was feeling himself entrapped in an un-canny intoxication. But we went on, searching through the misty gloom, through a bewildering maze of rocks. All the while the fog grew heavier and the chanting drummed into our ears—a de-mented song that now seemed to rise in a slow, wild crescendo.

This path, I thought, was leading us into the depths of Hell itself. This was no longer the land I knew, but a half-world reigned over by Satan. This way, I told myself, led to the home of his bestial children.

Suddenly we came upon a clearing. We were not certain at first that it was there because the pall of fragrance was so thick, so blinding. But through the enwrapping mist we saw naked bodies dancing in the shine of a great fire that was generating the smoke. It was a huge, smouldering mound across which avid tongues of flame licked—a heap, I saw of weeds. Fumes poured like a cascade into the hovering cloud above while, in the dim glow, the nude beings danced a dance of lust.

We beheld an obscene orgy that para-lyzed us with revulsion. We saw unfor-gettable vilenesses. We realized that this was the worship of the Mad Ones, this unspeakable mass evilness. It was every-where, so that when we tried to tear our protesting eyes from one insupportable sight, we saw another, then another. These were not human beings, we knew—no longer the friends we had known—but male and female demons performing rites

---

COMING SOON ---

THE RED EYE OF RIN-PO-CHE..................................Norvell W. Page
The wild heart of Moriarity O'Moore, gentlemen adventurer, yearned for a glamorous girl to fight for. His wish was answered, but he didn't expect to wage single-handed battle against a horde of men who brought to Broadway all the cruelty and treacherous wiles of the darkest jungles!

of abandoned lasciviousness. This was the altar and the temple of the Children of Satan.

AS we watched, a wild frenzy swept through the human beasts. They sprang up to run and gyrate, to chase and flee, to dance and shriek. In a moment the pit became a nightmare of madness. With the fog wreathing over us, shining opalescent in the flickering light of the flames, we stood in the shadow at the edge of the tumult. And Steve Heath, I knew, was searching among these beings of evil for the girl he loved.

Strange forces played over us, tricking our senses. The scene before our eyes seemed to recede, slowly but inexorably, until an unfathomable distance separated us from it. Should we travel all the days of our lives, I felt, through all the years of eternity, we could never reach the spot where the Devil's festival was occurring. Time itself became meaningless. Each second became an hour, each minute interminable. And all the while a kind of ecstasy grew in us, avid and terrible, urging us to fling ourselves into the orgy.

And, as suddenly, our senses twisted into other grotesqueries. A super-sensitiveness of perception swept over us. The crackling of the burning weeds became thunder in our ears. The dim light of the flames blinded us. The stifled cries of the Mad Ones stunned us like unbearably loud shouts. Our faintest sensations became spasms in their intensity. And all the while the evil ecstasy strengthened in us, threatening to overpower us, to claim us for this hellish revelry for ever. . . .

Then, on a prominence lifted above this scene of hellish revelry, I saw a figure— a motionless figure, its posture commanding, its presence kingly. In the wreathing of the smoke I could not be sure of its raiment, nor of its face, though I saw the gleaming of its eyes. If it were naked,

or if it were garbed, I could not know. But I was certain that this being was master of the fiendish festival, a lord of evil. I thought: this is Satan himself! This is Lucifer, clothed in flesh, looking upon his obscene brood. Before my eyes was the living Devil!

Suddenly I was conscious that one of the dancing figures had paused directly in front of Steve. The girl's nude body glistened in the writhing fog. Her widened eyes shone with an avid light. She had halted in her dance at sight of Steve, a beckoning smile on her lips, her whole body quivering with desire. She stepped toward him with a hungry whimper breaking through her loose lips. Her hands reached and her teeth shone.

It was Faith.

Her fingers closed on his arm. At the same instant, seized with terrified consternation, I grasped his other hand. "In God's name!" I shouted at him. "Come away! You'll never escape if you yield! She's no longer the girl you knew—she's a bestial fiend! Steve! Can you hear me? Come away! *Come away!*"

I tore him back. I thrust him into the rock-walled passage, prodded him into a run up the slope. He, too, realized the danger. He forced himself to go on, propelling his legs with all the strength of his will. Behind us, the girl followed. She loped. Her bare feet padded. We heard her panting breath. She thought, I knew, that Steve could not get away. I could almost feel her naked body weaving through the darkness after us.

We stumbled on the ledge. At the very brink we paused. Steve, looking back, saw her appear from the shadow. The gossamer of the smoke veiled around her. Her eyes gleaming with desire, she drifted toward him, arms outstretched. He tried to pull away from me, obsessed with the desire to fling himself into her deadly embrace; but I dared not let him beat me back. Suddenly, because in another moment she would claim him, I thrust him—into emptiness. . . .

THE girl shrieked her rage. The waters below broke violently with the impact of his body. Faith turned upon me in savage fury. To escape her clutch I flung myself after Steve. I plunged deep into the river, stroked up, then saw him striking out. Warm as the water was, it somehow served to clear our brains. We swam as we never had before, through an endless distance. When, at last, we reached the opposite bank, there was no chant pulsing through the air, no unearthly fog, but still we were afraid.

The island was the same dark mound in the glittering band of the river, clouded over with faintly opalescent mist.

Without speaking, we dressed. Together we followed the path back to the village. On the green great fires were burning—high heaps of twigs raging into white-hot coals. Around the blazes white-faced men and women were standing still as statues. These were biers, these fires. Biers for the Mad Ones whom the bullets of the militiamen had dropped. Soon they would be ashes. But when the Children of the Devil came again, I knew, more flames would leap up to consume the vile bodies of the doomed.

Even this sight did not give us pause, for only a few moments ago we had witnessed the ultimate abomination. I hurried into my house. At once I unlocked the closet in which I had imprisoned Erica. For a moment after the door was opened, she stood there motionless. Then, one arm behind her, she stepped out, smiling calmly.

"You see," she said, "I'm quite all right."

Was it Steve who was standing there in the room with us—this man of ashen face and defeated eyes and drawn mouth? Something frightful had happened to him inside. He looked utterly beaten, overwhelmed with despair. It was because everything dear to him had been destroyed—not merely destroyed, but transformed into a transcendent hideousness. He was thinking of Faith. . . . Faith, in that misty garden of Hell. . . .

I thought: let us face this, my friend. Let us acknowledge the horrible truth. This ghastliness which has consumed Faith is also our fate. How can we escape it? It has already inflicted its pestilence upon the whole village. It will claim us as it has claimed others—it will spread, a blight of Satan, until it plagues the entire world. Will we, then, be unlike others? No; we will be of them. In our mad vileness we will know no difference. Let us, then, my friend, not wrack ourselves with vain despair, for soon the doom will be upon us too.

A quick step on the porch disturbed us. We turned quickly, instantly alert. A rap followed. Steve warily opened the door, looked out. A small man with a fat face, exuding the odor of tobacco, quickly stepped in. He was Darrel Conger. He looked at us in a distraught manner, hesitating to speak when he saw Erica, but anguish forced it out of him. He blurted:

"There is one they didn't find. One that isn't being burned. She is behind the church. She must have lived a few seconds after the bullet hit her. She died there, near the spot where the bell was dug up. I didn't see her at first, but I found her because I was watching the doctor. He went there—he saw her. Now he's gone back."

I glanced at Erica. She was too bewildered to speak. I went to her, placed my automatic in her hand. "Keep it, Erica," I said. "Stay here—bolt yourself in—and use it if necessary. I'm going with

Steve. We—we've got to see what this means."

Darrel Conger had already shuffled out. Steve followed him. As I hurried after them, I heard Erica slide the bolt into the socket. At Steve's side, I hurried across the corner of the green, trying not to look at the flaring fires. Near the front of the town hall we saw a uniformed man standing rigidly, the light reflecting deeply in his eyes—Captain Delevan. Steve stepped to him at once.

"They're on the island," he said. "The Mad Ones. On the island. Do you understand?"

Delavan repeated with a blink: "The island? I can't go over there. That's outside the state. The state line runs down the middle of the river. The island's on the other side of it. I'll tell the Governor right away, and maybe we can get coöperation. The island, you say? How can you know that?" Then: "No matter where they come from, we'll wipe 'em out, sooner or later. It's my job to protect this village."

WE did not argue. We went on doggedly, silent. Moving into the shadow of the church, we paused. We could see it clearly, the girl's body sprawled there on the black ground. She was naked, lying as though peacefully asleep. Red had poured from a hole above her heart. The blood had streaked through the slime covering her legs. We stood there, looking at her without moving. Then our eyes lifted.

A door had opened on the slope of the hill behind the church. That low, squat building was the laboratory of Dr. Humphrey Bramwell. Its dipping eaves seemed always to give it a forbidding frown. Its windows, always closely blinded, hinted of secrets too terrible to be revealed to the light of day. At all hours of the night, we knew, it was the surgeon's habit to work at his mysterious tasks. A shaft of light had struck out of its open door, then had vanished.

Steps sounded. Dr. Humphrey Bramwell was approaching. Darrel Conger had seen him at the spot where the girl's body lay, and now he was coming back. He paused, looking around alertly, but he did not see us. We had taken care to retreat into the deepest shadow. Then, quickly, he stooped. He gathered the girl's dead body into his arms and held it close.

With the dead girl's body resting in his arms, Dr. Humphrey Bramwell hurried up the slope to his laboratory. We saw the door flash open, then shut. We gazed at each other revolted. Without speaking, but with grim, common accord, we hurried up the hill—Steve, Darrel Conger, and I.

Conger exclaimed under his breath: "Good God! It's not only a dead body he has claimed. Not only the lives of many who were our friends. He is destroying our whole village. It is dear to me. It has always been my home. I have believed in it. Every penny of my savings I have invested in the good earth inside the limits of Westmoorland." I knew this to be true, for I had negotiated many purchases of real estate for the tobacconist. "Now it is doomed to become a deserted town. It is becoming a part of Hell itself."

We noticed, as we climbed the slope, that even the ground on which the laboratory sat was different than the rest in that vicinity. It seemed black and rich, yet nothing grew on it. There was not a single blade of grass alive within many rods of the scientist's laboratory. It filled the air with a peculiar, pervading pungency. The slope on which the squat, mysterious building sat was like an earthy sore. Nothing lived near this structure in which a human devil had taken one who was dead—for what horrible purpose Satan himself only knew.

84

Very quietly Steve tried the door. It was fastened. We skirmished quietly along the side of the building. In a moment Steve was peering inward through a crack in one of the blinds, and I through another.

The girl's corpse lay on a wooden table, beneath the brilliant cone of a powerful bulb. Dr. Bramwell was bending over her. He had taken a large glass hypodermic syringe into his hand. Its needle glittered as he poised it. The slender steel sank into the flesh of the dead girl's thigh. Slowly, as we watched, the doctor drew out the plunger. Crimson welled into the barrel of the instrument—blood.

D R. Bramwell turned away, handling the syringe as though it were a thing exquisitely precious. At once he took up a bright implement of steel. It glinted brightly in the light, razor-edged, terrible. Again bending over the deceased girl, he made a quick, sure movement. The flesh opened beneath the hungry blade. We saw it part like bleeding lips crying out infinite pain.

More than this we could not endure. I straightened in horror to find Steve striding resolutely to the laboratory entrance. I was at his side when he knocked. The impact of his knuckles echoed with startling loudness beyond the door. After a moment of hush, the quick steps of Dr. Bramwell responded. He opened the door, looked out. He stepped through, closing it behind him. His eyes defiant, he asked: "Well, what do you want?"

Steve parried: "Shall I call Captain Delevan, doctor, to witness this ghastly thing you're doing?"

The surgeon stiffened. "If you wish," he said. "I will explain to him that I am exerting my utmost effort to find a serum to combat the madness. You have been spying on me, reading your own meaning into what you have seen, but you must admit that there is no other way to obtain a specimen of the blood of the inflicted. If I find the serum, it will save the rest of us. Then, I think, you will thank me—"

"All these years," Steve countered, "you have not been seeking a serum for this madness. From the beginning you have hidden yourself and concealed the nature of your work. God—or Satan—only knows what evils have transpired in this laboratory of yours. Your own son is the fountainhead of this blight. It has cost me the girl I love. I wonder, Dr. Bramwell, how much longer I can keep myself from killing you—"

The surgeon's bewhiskered lips curled. "I cannot undertake," he said acidly, "to justify myself to you. For a decade I have been making researches into the functionings of the endocrine system—the ductless glands. It is the new frontier of medicine, the closest we have come to the secret of personality, of life itself. That, being a layman, you cannot understand. And that, gentlemen, is all I have to say. Good night."

He stepped back, closing the door swiftly, shooting the bolt into its socket. So he imprisoned himself again with the dead girl. We were turning away, still trembling with revulsion, when we heard a low moan float up from the green. It was a prolonged lament that broke out suddenly, that swelled like a sad note of an organ. At once we hurried down the slope and turned toward the church.

Its doors had been flung open. We shouldered through the moaning crowd gathering from all over the village. We hurried up the aisle, into the gleam of the single candle burning on the altar—a taper guttering in a pool of molten wax, almost ready to extinguish itself. We gazed down at the horror that lay below the altar—all that remained of a man of God.

The face of the Reverend Matthew Middleton, always a visage of peaceful benignity, was now a misshapen red pulp. His blood had drenched him. He lay dead with a shotgun lying beside him— the weapon he had kept constantly at his side, since the first coming of the Mad Ones, to protect his house of worship. They had, at last, we knew now, penetrated into the church itself, and destroyed their master's enemy.

He had sacrificed his life during the tolling of the bell in the steeple. In the struggle, it was evident, an accidental discharge of the gun had taken his life. From him then, it was apparent, the demons had fled, for their lust was for the living— had fled from these holy walls, leaving the altar untouched. Perhaps some invisible barrier, which even the power of Satan could not penetrate, had stayed them.

The moaning rose in the church, a lament that lifted from the throats of the villagers. We turned back, stunned with grief, feeling that we had lost some of our strength to fight the scourge of madness. Militiamen were shouldering through the stricken crowd, ordering them to disperse, but none obeyed. We walked across the green, where mounds of coals were glowing, and returned to my house.

DARREL Conger left us to go to his shop. My knock admitted us to the room where Erica had imprisoned herself. We stood silent a moment, overwhelmed with hopelessness, wondering what new horror would next sweep upon us. I sensed something strange about Erica—saw some evasion in her eyes— and was about to question her concerning it when I glimpsed a movement of Steve's arm.

He lifted it, peeled back the cuff. I stared aghast at the ragged red indentations showing just above the wrist. The marks of human teeth held me transfixed a full moment. This was the stamp of madness. This was the brand of doom upon my dearest friend! Those marks of a demon's teeth. . . .

"I want you to know," Steve said quietly. "You and Erica—but no one else. None of them caught me. I haven't contracted the madness—yet. I did this to myself."

"You—?"

"If I went there," Steve said, "without the mark of teeth upon me, they would know. They would see at once that I am not one of them. They would fling themselves upon me—fill me with their horrible venom. This—" He gestured with the bitten wrist— "is my passport to hell."

I blurted: "You can't go back!"

"I'm going back," he said. "What is there left for me in this world? Faith is gone. She is there—with them. I belong with her. I think, perhaps, I can escape the madness, if I can make them believe I already have it. I can pretend it all. I can be near Faith, to watch over her.

Perhaps she will choose me, among all the others, because she once loved me. Whatever she has become I still love her. Yes, I am going back."

I gripped his arms. "You fool!" I snapped at him. "Do you think none of the rest of us love you? Don't you realize that life here, without Faith, empty as it must be, is better than—that? It's too late, Steve! You can't save her now! She's gone—gone forever. And if you go, you'll sink with her. The things you'll see, there in that living hell—they'll eat your soul away. The horrors all around you—they'll rot you. Good God, Steve, I can't let you do this! I can't let you go!"

"I'm going," he said, "to Faith. When the bell tolls again, I'm going."

I knew then that he must.

CHAPTER FOUR

The Voice of Satan

THERE was no sunset that day. Throughout the light hours the sky hung oppressively low, pregnant with storm. Twilight came as a time of ominous hush, as though all the forces of creation had ceased. Then, as the darkness thickened, a wind began to flow out of the horizon, steadily, strengthening. Far in the distance thunder rumbled and lightning sparkled behind floating, mountainous blackness. But, soul-stifling oppression that this was, it was nothing compared with the storm which gathered that day in the hearts of men.

I heard the whispers passing from villager to villager as they gathered on the green, speaking in low tones, furtively. I heard the name of Dr. Bramwell pronounced. Men spat after speaking it. They turned baneful eyes toward the laboratory on the hill behind the church. From house to house the messages carried, like an invisible fire of hatred. They were planning, I knew—planning to destroy this monster, this living Satan, this spreader of abomination. They were banding together to cast him back into the depths of Hell. . . .

I felt the power of their purpose growing throughout the day; and when darkness came, with the storm rumbling in the angry heavens, I sensed that the explosion of wrath might come at any moment. I did not tell Erica of this. She did not speak of it, though I felt she knew. She remained at my house with Steve, strangely silent. And Steve was waiting grimly, even impatiently, for the coming of midnight, hoping that the bell would toll—toll to signal him to Faith's side in the Mad Ones' Hell on earth.

A driving desperation filled me, reaching an intensity after dark that would not let me rest. Goaded with anxiety, I left the house. Crossing the green, I saw burned scars, mounds of ashes which the rising wind was eddying into the air. The storm was rapidly approaching, rolling out of the distance. Soon it would cross the river and unleash its fury upon the village of the doomed.

It was late when I hurried to the church. During the day its doors and windows had been covered with boards, firmly nailed. This was a defiance to the Children of Satan, an attempt to preserve the sanctity of our place of worship against their evil invasions. I had helped cover the colored glass portraits of the saints, and during that task I had noticed something strange. I had not investigated then, but a memory of it tantalized me. Now, late as the hour was, near as it was to midnight, I went back to examine this thing.

Nearing the church I paused, seeing squads of militiamen standing at attention before their commander. Captain Delevan's orders had summoned them from their posts. I was at first alarmed because he had removed them from their watchful positions on the roofs, from their patrols in the streets. Then I realized that he had determined upon some new and more desperate tactic—this officer who, I felt, was far shrewder than he wished anyone to believe. He seemed about to command them into action. I stepped to his side.

"Captain Delevan," I said, "I think I have found something important. I'm not quite sure what it may mean, but it's worth investigating. It will take only a few moments to show you what I found this afternoon while helping board the windows of the church. Will you come?"

He hesitated, scrutinizing me, then ordered his men to stand at ease. He kept glancing at his strap-watch as we strode into the churchyard. The wind whipped around us and the lightning of the approaching storm glared intermittently while I led him to the wall of the church. I struck a match and cupped it, but instantly its flame was torn away. Delevan brought a flashlight from his pocket and turned its beam upon a spot I indicated.

"Wires," I said. I ran my fingers along them. "They are carefully concealed at the side of the window frame, you see. They run from above—from the belfry, possibly. This is not a telephone line, nor a power lead. I don't know what it is, but it's highly suspicious. . . . I think we should trace these wires."

Delevan's eyes sharpened. The spot of his light smeared down the old clapboards to the ground. The wires, he found, disappeared into the earth. He pulled on them carefully, tore them up from the sod. We followed them, foot by foot, across the yard. Soon we paused, at the door of an old shed sitting at the rear of the rectory. The wires led inside. Delevan opened the way. We stepped into musty darkness broken only by the beam of the captain's torch.

IT played upon an accumulation of old furniture, across an ancient buggy, upon stacks of firewood and a chopping block, through cobwebs, over a bed of woodchips, loose earth and dust. We followed the wires, always pulling on them to draw them out of their concealment, along the wooden wall. Presently, in the rear corner, we discovered that they led to an ancient trunk and disappeared through a hole drilled into it. We pried the lid open.

For a moment we stared at the device which Captain Delevan's torch revealed. He blinked in wonderment. The bottom of the trunk was filled with storage batteries, interconnected to a contrivance supported on brackets above them. Part of this contraption was a clock mechanism. There was a small motor worm-geared to a cylinder which, when revolving, comprised a make-and-break contact. We saw, too, that the alarm hand of the clock was set precisely to the hour of midnight.

The rising wind slapped upon the old shed as the captain and I examined this machine. The air quaked with bursts of thunder, each louder, more violent than the last. Brilliant flashes of lightning gleamed in through the cracks of the trembling walls like a lacework of fire. The storm was sweeping hard upon the village. But we were scarcely aware of it as we studied the strange contrivance.

Delevan said slowly: "I know what this does. This is only half of the whole arrangement. The other half must be concealed in the bell in the belfry—a strong magnet. This device sends powerful impulses of electricity into the magnet. Each time the drum revolves, contact is made, and the clapper hits the bell. This is what makes the bell ring."

We stared at each other, with the growing roar of the storm beating around us, but we were deaf to it. We were listening to the ticking of the clock. Its pulsant voice chilled us. It was turning the release mechanism slowly but inevitably

88

toward midnight. At the stroke of the hour of evil, we knew, this hidden motor would begin to whir and, up in the old steeple, the hellish bell would begin its clamor.

"It's set to ring tonight—in only a few minutes!" I exclaimed. "It will bring the Mad Ones!"

Captain Delevan nodded. I thrust my cold hands inside the trunk. I caught hold of the two wires connecting with the drum. With one sharp, snapping pull I tore them away. I destroyed the circuit leading to the bell. I straightened grimly, eyes fixed upon the captain.

"Now it won't ring!" I said. "That damned bell won't toll tonight. It will never raise its voice again. We've found the secret—we've silenced it. Thank God we did it in time! A few minutes more, and the bell would have started. But now it can't. It will never ring again!"

Delevan looked grim. "I don't understand this," he said, "but I want to know who made this machine. This shed is on the church grounds, but certainly the minister had nothing to do with it. He couldn't have known anything about it. Someone else did it—someone who sneaked in here now and then to wind the clock and charge the batteries when they ran down. I want to know—"

"I think—" I began.

The same thought gleamed in his eyes. We stepped from the shed. Rain whipped down. It came suddenly, thickly, great splashing drops pelting viciously. The furious wind gusted at us. Crashing thunder dinned in our ears. Lightning flared, followed by another deafening concussion. We scarcely noticed. We gazed up the slope at the low building whose windows were ominously blinded.

"It's the closest," Captain Delevan said through the mounting uproar. "The laboratory of Dr. Humphrey Bramwell. Only a few seconds away. Look here—we've

got to be careful. We have no proof that he did it. Flatly accusing him will get us nowhere. We've got to watch him— catch him at the right moment, committing an incriminating act. When the bell doesn't ring at midnight, as it was set to do, he may sneak down to see what's wrong. I want you to keep your eye on this shed."

"But you?" I asked.

"We can't take any chances," he answered. "Those crazy devils from the island may come without the bell ringing this time. We can't be sure they won't. Anyway, I have my orders to follow. I can't abandon my men. Our job is to keep those hell-fiends back if we can. It's only a few more minutes until midnight now. You watch this place while I go through with my plan. Have you a gun?"

My automatic was in my pocket.

"Good," he said. "If anyone shows up, stop at nothing to capture him. Shoot him down, if you need to. God knows he deserves a bullet in the heart, but be careful not to kill him. We've got to learn his story—get a full confession. You understand?"

THE captain turned away at my nod. He strode off toward the green. I stepped under the little roof of the side door of the church to evade the rain, but I could not escape it. The cascade from the black heavens was being ripped and hurled by the terrific wind so that no open shelter could keep it out. It beat against the church. A whining and creaking came from the belfry, like cries of torture, as it swayed in the power of the storm. Again and again eye-stinging lightning glared and the drums of thunder rolled mightily as I stood there, watching. . . .

While the storm howled its fury, while I stood there drenched, automatic in hand, I heard the tramp of marching feet. Looking across the green, I saw the militia trudging off into the darkness. They were moving toward the river. I realized, then, that Captain Delevan was making a wise, strategic deploy. He was intent on scattering his men along the bank, to cut off the approach of the Mad Ones if they should come, and in that way keep them from reaching the village.

They marched on, vanishing behind the curtains of sluicing rain, and on until even the beat of their boots blended away into the thunderous turmoil.

Thank God, I told myself, the bell is silenced!

Then I became aware of a concerted movement on the green. I peered from the church door to see men and women springing from their homes, unmindful of the deluge. Immediately their clothing flattened against their bodies and streamed, but they gave no notice. They were moving with a grim intensity of purpose. Some of them hurried into sight carrying torches. The reddish flare of the flames glittered through the downpour. I saw weapons in their hands—axes, cleavers, knives, rifles, pistols, clubs. They came from everywhere, a silent mob, to gather on the green. And all their gleaming eyes turned toward the laboratory of Dr. Humphrey Bramwell.

They crowded there with the storm beating over them. They were waiting, I knew—waiting for the stroke of midnight, for the evil bell to raise its hideous voice. They had reached the limit of their endurance. They had seen their daughters and sons defiled. They had seen their man of God sacrifice his life. They had suffered insupportably. Now they were possessed with the purpose of destroying the author of these evils.

During those few minutes the fury of the heavens reached a pitch of transcendant violence. Rain sheeted savagely. Eye-burning streaks of lightning lanced the sky, drilled down into the woods. The very earth quaked with the cosmic force of the thunder. But the mob stood there, weapons in their hands, torches flaring in spite of the deluge, waiting, peering at the dwelling of their dread enemy.

My watch read midnight.

Then the bell tolled!

ITS first vibrant stroke beat resonantly through the turmoil of the storm like a fiendish cry. The second pulsant tone followed quickly. The reverberations quickened into a demoniacal uproar. The voice of the bell shouted and shrieked through the crashing of the tempest. Its metallic scream reached far through the sodden, churning night.

It is the wind ringing the bell. . .! The wind!

A mournful cry broke from the throats of the mob on the green. The lament rose into a howl of rage. Savage fury rang in the discordant chorus as the crowd started forward. They broke into a loping run across the green. They began swarming around the church, sweeping up the slope toward the laboratory of Dr. Bramwell. Their crazy cries carried shrilly through the surging of the storm.

"Kill him Burn him! Drive him back to hell! Destroy the devil! Burn him! Kill him!"

Then, adding to the frantic tumult of the night, the cracking of rifles from afar! The weapons of the militia barking. This the howling mob did not hear, but I caught the rattling of the fusilades through the withering savagery of the storm. It meant that the Mad Ones were stampeding across the river. The Mad Ones were coming!

The mob of villagers swept upon the laboratory of Dr. Bramwell. They surrounded it, brandishing their weapons. They attacked its windows and its locked door. In their frenzy they even beat upon its hated walls with their fists. Inside that structure, I knew, the surgeon was trapped. Soon they would reach him. Soon they would fasten their vengeful hands upon him and rend the living Satan!

I saw two figures racing through the downpour—a man and a girl. In the gleam of the torches I glimpsed Steve Heath's face and Erica's. I knew they had seen the mob gather on the green. They were flinging themselves through the sluicing downpour toward the laboratory. Until then I had held my station, watching the shed which contained the hidden mechanism. I broke away, sprinting after them.

The bell tolled! It clamored! It dinned out its brazen voice! It deafeningly called its message of evil—shrieking its signal to the Mad Ones.

I sped to the laboratory. I saw Erica fighting her way through the milling crowd, striving to reach the entrance. A huge, powerful-shouldered man was driving the blade of an axe into it. While windowpanes splintered under the beating cudgels of the others, this man crashed his axe into the door. The panels were cracking out. In a moment it would be broken down. Through it, white in the brilliant light of the laboratory, I saw the haggard face of the surgeon.

Erica flung herself on the man who was whipping the axe against the entrance. She struggled to tear it from his hands. Others seized her arms and shoulders, attempting to wrench her away, but she clung desperately. I hastened toward her, intent only on freeing her, if possible, from the fury of the mob. But as I groped through the torrent I glimpsed Steve Heath standing drenched on the slope, peering toward the river.

New cries were ringing through the raging darkness. It was a mad, lustful chant growing louder, louder. It swept swiftly closer, from all points at once. Then, through the lashing rain, I glimpsed naked bodies glistening. Girls and men were running wantonly out of the saturated gloom, swarming upon the village. I knew then that not even the rifles of the militia had stayed the invasion. The Mad Ones were upon us.

Steve, unmindful of his own danger, hurried into their very midst. He was, I knew, seeking Faith. No one but he and I, I felt, knew that the Children of Satan had come again. They herded across the slope, but the mob of villagers was so frenziedly intent upon destroying the living Satan that they did not notice the shining wet bodies, the glaring eyes, the gleaming teeth. Madness upon madness flooded through the night.

Erica! I saw her being held, pulled back from the door. Again the axe flashed up, cleaved hard into the wood. Another man, wielding a sledge hammer, smashed its weighty head against the frame of the broken door. It crashed inward. At once a treble howl broke from the throats of the avengers. They flung themselves into the laboratory—but it was Erica, frantically pulling herself free, who sprang in first.

Sprang in to her father, whirled at his side to defy the rage of the villagers. She cried, "Go back! Go back!" She lifted her arm as though to forbid them to advance. At that second I forgot everything in the world except Erica—the frenzy of my neighbors, even the evil, raiding Mad Ones. I saw nothing but Erica, her one arm uplifted. I stared in a paralysis of horror.

The flesh of her arm was broken with the marks of human teeth!

A CHOKING shout broke from my lips. I fought wildly past the men and women massing in the laboratory. I struggled to Erica's side, caught her arm, stared at the brand. It was there—the indentations of human teeth, a small curved line that had bitten through her skin—the mark of doom.

I scarcely heard the raging of the storm and the clamor of the crowd.

Darrel Conger had fought his way to the side of Dr. Bramwell. With a revolver in his hand he was facing the mob. For a moment it brought them to a standstill. Conger's other hand, I saw, was poised, and dripping blood. Like Erica's arm—though his mark was fresher—it bore the bite of human teeth. One glance was enough for any of us to realize that a Mad One had seized upon him outside the laboratory. He gazed silently, compassionately, at Erica.

Then, with chilling suddenness, the lights went out. Perhaps one of the axes, still chopping at the walls, had severed the lines. Perhaps the storm had brought down the wires. Reasons meant nothing to us at that moment. The lights went out with paralyzing abruptness, filling the laboratory with suffocating darkness. For a moment there was no movement. Then a low, growling chant rose—a note of anger. The villagers began groping through the gloom, seeking their victim, the doctor.

"Erica!" I called. "Erica!"

No answer came from her. There was maddening pandemonium everywhere, but not a whisper of Erica's voice. As I fought my way to the spot where I had last seen her, I heard Dr. Bramwell bellow her name—a call voicing terror. I brushed against him. I gripped his arm. At that moment I was startled to feel a strong gust of wind. Turning, I saw a door at the rear of the laboratory flying open. Two dark figures darted through it, into the downpour—and vanished.

"Erica!"

Dr. Bramwell tore free of my grip. I sprang to the open door. The villagers were blinded, struggling with each other in their crazed confusion. I was able to shoulder my way out. As I sprang into the pelting rain, I heard someone running

beside me. A flash of lightning revealed Dr. Bramwell plunging along with great, heavy strides. In my fury I bounded at him. I gripped his arms, forced him to a standstill.

Before I could speak he thundered at me: "Don't stop me! By God, man, if you try to stop me, I'll kill you! Someone has taken Erica. He's dragging her toward the river. Listen! Can't you hear her calling? If you love her, help me bring her back! Help me!"

He wrenched himself free again, flung himself through the storm with that awkward, apelike lope of his. In an instant my estimation of Dr. Bramwell was transformed. I knew his plea was sincere. Regardless of all else he might have done, no matter what vileness he had perpetrated, he was frantically anxious for Erica's safety. Mad or not, in that I could and must join him. In a moment I found myself running through the sluicing rain at the side of that huge, strange man.

Only flickering flashes of lightning showed us the way. The roar of the storm drummed constantly in our ears, though the crazy hubbub of the villagers and the shrieking of the Mad Ones was left behind. With Dr. Bramwell I stumbled to a stop on the bank of the lashing river. A flare of lightning showed us that no one was near—but out in the water, someone was swimming. Two vague figures—I could see them, the waves lashing over their heads. One, I knew, must be Erica—Erica being claimed for Satan's Eden.

I plunged into the water. Dr. Bramwell dove in near me. He struck out with amazing strength, beating the water with fast, sure strokes. I needed all my strength to keep up with him. We fought wind and waves, peered through blinding rain. By the time we were half across that fury of water, Erica had vanished. She had, I knew, already reached the island. With the one who had seized her, she was being forced even now into the vile service of her Satanic master.

I kicked myself to the rocks, climbed up. Dr. Bramwell heaved after me. We came breathless to the ledge. A heavy, heady scent pervaded the air—the incense which even the storm could not wash out of the atmosphere. It was coming from a smouldering fire which, I knew, the deluge could not quench. Even in this tempest the smudge of Satan was burning. We started along the path, the intoxicating fragrance growing thicker at each step. We went down farther and farther, between ominous walls, toward the heart of that hell on earth.

"Listen!" I cautioned. "Hear them! The Mad Ones are coming back! Hurry!"

WE stumbled to a stop at the edge of the fearful hollow. Fumes were churning in the air from the heap of weeds. Now the fiends' arena was empty —but the Mad Ones were coming back. We saw, in that drenched haze, no movement for a moment. Then my eyes lifted to the prominence on which I had seen the strange, unworldly figure who reigned over the Children of Satan. He was there —the master of evil.

We could see little—only enough to be sure the presence was upon his stony throne—that he was not alone. I sprang away, following a rugged path that wound and rose to the shelf. Dr. Bramwell panted after me. He shouldered through a narrow opening between two rocks, and stopped appalled. In the thick haze our vision was untrustworthy, but still we could see. Erica—Erica poised like a queen on the rock, her clothing stripped off, her naked body wreathed with smoke and streaming with rain.

A man was crouched beside her—or a human devil. His hands were fastened avidly upon her. Her wide, shining eyes were directed down at him. The back of this being was turned upon us. We sprang toward him. There was murder in our hearts. We were hungry to kill this devil who had cast a spell of evil upon our village, who now had claimed Erica. We sprang. He straightened, spun about. A snarl of rage broke through his drawn lips. He leaped with the agility of a jungle beast. Dr. Bramwell and I bounded after him. We forced him between us, closed him in. He fought madly, savagely, screaming, howling with consummate rage. His wet body slipped from our wet hands. He squirmed away, but we hurled ourselves on him again. We forced him down—down into the fuming embers of the fire of hell.

"Damn you, Darrel Conger!" Dr. Bramwell choked out. "Damn you!"

A plaintive cry broke from behind us. I turned to find Erica groping through the mist. The madness was upon her, but some faint spark of sanity was left—a glow that was leading her toward us for safety. She sprang to my side, and clung to me, her body shining in the smouldering gleam and trembling. Dr. Bramwell straightened, his huge hands clamped upon Conger. We listened—listened to the padding of many running feet, to an inarticulate muttering, a clashing of teeth. They were coming—coming. . . .

The Mad Ones were upon us. They had swarmed back across the river, climbed again into their reeking haven. They sprang into view from rocks and trees, hordes of them, all craven, lustful human beasts. They caught sight of us in the radiance of the scattered fire. They came closer, like stalking beasts, their eyes avid, their gleaming teeth bared. The human pack was closing in, marking us for their victims, their hungry fangs moist with horrible poison. Hands groping, from all around us they came.

I blurted: "Behind us—the slope!"

The torrential rain was spilling down an earthy, rock-studden incline that rimmed part of the hollow. There alone lay a path of retreat from the Mad Ones. I tightened my arm around Erica, forced her to run at my side. She moved with animal-like nimbleness, her nudeness veiled by the banked smoke. Dr. Bramwell, clenching Conger's arm, beat the tobacconist into a stumbling climb. We flung ourselves higher and higher, through mud that clung to our feet like leaden weights, through foaming water that churned white in the gloom.

Suddenly other groups bounded into sight almost in our path. They had skirted ahead, swift as predatory wolves, to cut us off. We saw the glittering of the water beyond—water promising a way of escape—but the Children of Satan were barring the way. The rain whipped, the mud oozed under their feet, as they sealed the circle around us. Erica clung to me closely, Dr. Bramwell kept his grip on Conger, as the hellish ring grew tighter, tighter. . . .

Suddenly the booming, commanding tones of the scientist broke through the tumult of the storm.

"Look at this man!" The power of his muscles lifted Conger, raised him before the hungry eyes. "This is the man who called himself your king! This is one you worshipped! But look! He is afraid—afraid of you! His power is gone! You are no longer his slaves—he is yours! The king is fallen! The king is no more! Take him! *Take him!*"

DR. Bramwell thrust Conger with a mighty power that sent the tobacconist stumbling down the slope. The slippery earth beneath Conger, the driving whip of the rain, forced him into a crazy, screaming run. He tottered toward the groping hands of the Mad Ones. He reeled into an insane attempt to escape them—but he could not. They sprang upon him all at once, as though they all were a part of the same fiendish hunger. Conger's terrorized cries were muted by the shrilling of the human beasts. They hurled themselves upon him with insane ferocity.

For a moment the three of us on the slope were forgotten in favor of the closer prey of the Mad Ones. It was an instant's respite upon which Dr. Bramwell had gambled, upon which all our hope of escape depended. I gripped Erica's arm, pulled her away. Dr. Bramwell rushed with us over the crest, down toward the river. It was lashing and whipping violently in the wind. We plunged into it, dragging Erica with us.

With all our strength we fought the current toward the opposite bank. I was ready to seize Erica if she should attempt to turn back. Nearing the foamy edge of the water, I gripped her arm again and pulled her up.

She stumbled along between Dr. Bramwell and me. Our only thought was to find shelter for Erica. The besieged laboratory was not possible. The green of the village was still swarming when we skirted along behind the houses. We circled to my door. I thrust it wide, forced Erica through. Her father staggered in with her. I turned, at the sound of chorused voices. Figures were moving close.

Steve Heath, white-faced, was fighting his way toward the house. His one arm was around a girl who was almost nude —Faith. He had found her, was struggling to bring her back. I hurried to aid him. Gripping Faith's arms, we hurried her into the house. I was closing the door when, peering dazed at the church tower rising into the holocaust, I saw the wrath of Heaven strike.

At that instant the fury of the firmament reached its cataclysmic peak. A blinding bolt of lightning shot down from the sky. It drove its power into the steeple of the church. Soaring flame burst out. Splintered wood shrieked as it yielded to the force striking out of the tempest. The old belfry tottered. It broke at its base. It plunged to the ground with a resounding, earth-wracking concussion, carrying with it the devil's bell.

A last, vibrant, piercing note shrieked from the unholy bell, then even the storm was hushed. . . .

* * *

I have before me the report of Dr. Almon Rockman, director of the state prison for the criminally insane, concerning the case of Darrel Conger. It reveals the amazing truths behind the evil the tobacconist spawned. To the examiners Conger confessed the plan that he built up soon after the finding of the old church records in the library of the rectory.

He was apparently a quiet, homely figure, this tobacconist, but within him lived a consuming avarice. He had discovered, in the old records, something which he hoped might bring him great riches. This man, toiling by day at his bench, fashioning cigarettes and cigars, dreamed of himself as a Croesus. The secret he learned placed riches almost within his grasp.

He knew the reason why the buried bell had never tarnished, why no grass grew on the slope to Dr. Bramwell's laboratory —why, in fact, the fires of Hell spoken of by the ancient, Daniel Warlaw, had appeared. In the days when those records were written no one knew what petroleum was. It was a time of whale-oil lamps, long before any automobile had ever been conceived. The seepage in the soil around the old church had revealed to Conger that a vast reservoir of oil might lay beneath it.

This was the reason why, using me as his real estate agent, he had saved every penny to buy land. But the most vital parcels he could not purchase. Dr. Bramwell would not consider selling the site of the laboratory, and the plot on which the church stood was inviolate. Frustrated by this, Conger had contrived to gain his ends in the only possible way—by emptying the town, by destroying it so that, later, he could claim the wealth lying hidden under the crust of the earth.

Conger knew, as none of the rest of us did, that a certain weed grew wild in the district, as it does in many parts of the United States—marijuana. This is the plant sometimes known as the "killer weed", the same that produces in the Far East the narcotic called hasheesh. With it Conger had combined a plant which grows wild in India, called Dhara, a powerful aphrodisiac. None of us knew, until the psychiatrists' report, that Conger, on the one trip abroad that he had taken in his younger days had, because of his deep interest in herbs, brought back the seeds of this flower. He had grown it in his garden behind his shop. By the use of these two drugs, blended into his tobaccos, he was able to put his daring plan into operation—the creation of the Mad Ones.

CONGER is serving a life sentence in the state asylum for the insane, while the Mad Ones are no more. Their treatment under Dr. Bramwell is progressing rapidly. Both Faith and Erica made quick recoveries. The scientist's patient ministrations have revealed him in an entirely new light to the villagers who, regretful of their misunderstanding of him, now almost worship him. My own error of judgment has led me to hold the doctor in the highest esteem—as, indeed, I should, since he will soon become my father-in-law.

Yet, deep in my heart, I feel that Conger's confession, complete as it is, somehow fails to tell the whole truth—fails because no man could know it all. I am haunted by the fact that its bed of earth cannot shut away the power of the bell.

For, once the bell crashed from its tower during the storm, as though struck down by the hand of God. it was again sunk into a hollow and covered. There it shall remain, even though excavations are made to tap the reservoir of oil beneath the church. Until the day of doom it will rest there, a thing of evil, still a symbol that none of us can forget—a mystery which not even Conger's revelations can dispel.

It was not the tobacconist who cast the bell. The story which old Daniel Warlaw told us has not changed. The bell tolled out evil, and evil there will always be. The blood and the soul of a woman of evil are imprisoned forever in the metal. Whatever else may be true, it was her voice calling, the tolling of that bell—her cry to her mate.

And Satan came. . . .

THE END

96